Behind the Wall

Behind the Wall

The untold true story of how a truck driver's wife
united Australia's national trucking industry

Written by Lights on the Hill Founder

KATHY WHITE OAM

First published in Australia in 2025

by Kathleen White

Copyright © Kathleen White 2025

ISBN 978-0-9925769-8-1

Cover design by Bettina Kaiser art + design

Formatting by coeurdelion.com.au

A catalogue record for this book is available from the National Library of Australia

Thank you to these special people:

Kevin Saxby
Neil (Dusty) Fraser
Sharon Andrews
Travis Sinclair
Ian Pearse
Jim McDonald
Christine Eggins
Debbie Thompson
Hope Burrows
Kilah family
Garry White
Dionne White
Tracy O'Shea
The music artists who contributed to the CDs and sang on stage at every event; the people who attended the convoys, memorials, and fundraisers who donated to Lights On The Hill.
Volunteers
Truck drivers and their friends and families.

A NOTE ABOUT AUSTRALIA'S TRUCKING INDUSTRY

Driving a truck in Australia is this country's deadliest job.

Monash University data[1] reveals truck drivers are 13 times more likely to die at work than any other profession. Being a truck driver is one of the unhealthiest career paths out there thanks to long hours, social isolation, time pressure and lack of job control. Not to mention dreadful eating.

Official data show annual deaths in crashes involving any heavy truck (including articulated trucks and heavy rigid trucks)[2]:

- March 2020 – 175
- March 2021 – 167
- March 2022 – 175
- March 2023 – 179
- March 2024 – 183

That is 879 deaths on Australian roads in the past five years and the numbers aren't reducing.

These statistics are horrendous. Life as a truck driver is like a roulette wheel. As one driver said to me once: "You never know when or if you will get home safe. If you do get home, you appreciate you made it home, and head out to face it all again the next day".

1   https://www.monash.edu/medicine/news/latest/2018-articles/monash-study-most-dangerous-job

2   https://www.bitre.gov.au/sites/default/files/documents/heavy_bulletin_mar2024.pdf

A long-distance truck driver is on the roads every day at work. Most people go to and from work, so there is a big difference in 'time spent' on the roads as a professional driver. Even sales people have a break from the road, but a truck driver must find a place to pull over to be able to sleep. The hardest things to find are a place to eat, a clean place for a shower and a decent toilet.

Truck drivers miss their kids growing up; they miss a lot of special moments in life. The partner at home must act as both parents, because the other is on the road – day in, day out.

I know, I have done this.

Over my years involved with trucks, I have heard many terrible stories. I know of people jumping in front of trucks; they park on the side of the road just waiting to drive under a truck. I know of a truck driver who hung himself from his steps in a high-set house – he couldn't cope with life after a car flew out from a side street. Young children the same age as his kids were killed in the crash and he could not cope with what he saw.

News travels fast in the trucking industry. We received so many phone calls from friends telling us of other friends who had been killed in trucks. When I was running the Lights on the Hill (LOTH) trucking memorial wall, I used to receive up to three calls in one day, sometimes daily, telling me about a truck driver who had been killed. One lady, who had lost her husband and son in truck accidents, called me to have her second (and last) son put on the memorial wall. "He was killed last night," she said. Well, we both cried together, I felt so sorry for this lady, as I did for all the families I helped to place their loved ones on the wall. Each loss showed how the drivers face dangers every day.

One driver I put on the wall died from a car hitting him when he was changing his tyre; another was killed when someone broke into his truck while he was trying to sleep. A $5 note was stolen from his wallet, and he lost his life in trying to defend himself.

One driver went missing – his truck was found with the door open, and he just disappeared; his clothes and wallet were still in the truck.

Here is an example of what drivers' face. My husband, Garry, was taking fuel to Armidale in the northern tablelands of New South Wales, and he was having a sleep in the cab of the truck. Some kids took the fire extinguisher – the police found the tag from the extinguisher in one of the kid's pockets. They tried to light a match at the outlets where the fuel was released to fill the service stations. Luckily they couldn't work out where the release valve was for the fuel, and when that didn't work, would you believe they took an electric fence from the side of the road to wrap around the tanker? Eventually, they decided to rob the driver. Garry woke up as soon as they stepped up on the truck step. He grabbed one of the boys' arms and went out of the cab in his undies, still holding this kid.

Can you imagine if that truck was set alight it would have exploded along with the entire service station, killing the kids, my husband and torching homes and businesses for several kilometres. It would have probably flattened half the town. After that night I was scared every time my husband left home. I didn't stress about anything until that horrible night. The kids' punishment was to write a letter to say they were sorry.

When you are married to a truck driver, you never know if they are going to come home. You're just grateful every time they do.

Road fatalities are reported in the media. But the vast majority of accidents go unreported. We don't hear that a truck driver will never walk again, or has lost their legs, or an arm. There are many truck drivers out there who will never drive a truck again because of injuries or trauma, of either witnessing an accident or being involved in one.

One day, when I had my Lights on the Hill shirt on, a family came up to me and said they hated trucks and the drivers; their friend was killed in a truck accident. My reply was that my friend's entire family was killed in a two-car collision. And another was killed by a car while riding a push bike. Accidents happen every day. Trucking accidents are not a reason to hate truck drivers, just as car accidents are not a reason to hate cars.

In my opinion, when everyone gets a driver's licence they should have to know the lengths of a truck, and how long it takes for a truck to stop. Many times, I have been in the cab of a truck, and we have left space between us and the vehicle in front, only to have another car pull in front of us.

I recall two memorable incidents of trucks turning left and having to use the right-hand lane to do this manoeuvre, simply because of their size. A lady car driver who had to deliver a wedding cake saw the left-hand lane was free. She said, "I thought I had enough time to get past on the inside lane". No, she didn't. She was now in a spot where truck drivers can't see vehicles beside them. The truck went around the corner and over the bonnet of the lady's car. The cake and the driver survived the crash but she didn't get to the wedding on time. My husband was the driver of the truck.

Another time, a lady car driver was in a hurry to pick up her child from school one day. There were three semi-tippers in the right-hand lane, each with blinkers on to turn left. She thought if she went fast enough, she would beat us. The first truck went around the corner, followed by the second one, that was halfway around the corner. This little white car got stuck between the wheels and was dragged around the corner. I closed my eyes; I didn't want to see this woman squashed. The only way we could get her car out was to lift the tipper a few times. By the time they could get the car out from under the trailer, it was squashed. She survived, just. This lady, who was in such a hurry to pick up her child, was now extremely late. A police officer went to collect her child. Did the police have a go at the lady? Yes they did.

In my opinion, there would be fewer accidents if drivers were tested on every licence test about trucks needing the right-hand lane to turn left, and the safe stopping distances trucks need to stop.

One of the worst things that can happen to truck drivers is when people think they can beat a truck. I can name quite a few people who have been killed by vehicles shooting out onto a highway from a side street. They forget that the truck is probably doing 100 kmh on open roads, and they cannot stop just because people think if they hurry they will beat this truck. I have been in the truck as a passenger and had several close calls like this. It is sickening, and leaves you shaking for several hours later.

Here are my three hopes for the future of the Australian trucking industry:

1 **Better understanding of trucking**

Driving a truck in Australia is not just a job. It's a relentless battle against time, fatigue, and the constant threat of danger. The statistics alone are sobering. But the numbers don't tell the whole story. Behind every statistic is a driver, a family, a community shattered by loss. Truck drivers face unimaginable challenges daily: long hours, physical and emotional isolation, and the perpetual risk of accidents. For those of us who have lived this life or loved someone who has, it's not just about the logistics or the pay cheque. It's about survival, resilience, and often, a heavy toll on mental health and family life.

2 **Shared responsibility on the roads**

The relationship between truck drivers and other road users is fraught with misunderstanding and, at times, hostility. Many drivers don't realise the unique challenges trucks face – turning, stopping distances or blind spots. These gaps in awareness can lead to devastating accidents. Education is key. If everyone obtaining a driver's license was required to understand the basics of truck dynamics, such as the space needed to stop or manoeuvre, we could prevent countless tragedies. Truck drivers are not the enemy; they are professionals navigating massive vehicles in conditions most of us would find overwhelming. Road safety is a shared responsibility that demands patience, respect, and awareness from all road users.

3   Hope for change

While the stories of loss and danger in trucking are heart-wrenching, they also highlight the urgent need for systemic change. Better support for truck drivers – be it through safer working conditions, improved rest facilities, or mental health resources – can save lives. But it's not just about the industry; it's about fostering understanding and empathy on the road. Every safe trip home, every life spared from a preventable accident, is a victory. For truck drivers, their families, and everyone who shares the road with them, this change is not just necessary—it's long overdue. Let's honour their work and sacrifices by making their lives, and our roads, safer for all.

Kathy White OAM, Maaroom Queensland

Prologue

One spring morning, a lady arrived at the memorial wall and saw another lady sitting in front of it, looking deep in thought.

"Hi, may I sit beside you? I won't disturb you."

"Of course you can, you can disturb me as much as you like."

She smiled and looked at the front of the wall. "My husband is on this wall; do you have anyone on the wall, my dear?" she asked.

"Yes, sadly."

"I would love to know the history of this beautiful memorial wall, wouldn't you?"

"Well, if you have plenty of time, I can tell you the history of this project."

"That would be wonderful, thank you. I have plenty of time because I'm retired now due to ill health, so I'm all ears. I want to hear everything you know, the good and the bad."

"It's a long story. Are you sure you have time?"

"Yes dear, I want to know how and why this wall was built. My name is Milly, by the way."

"Nice to meet you Milly, I'm Kathy."

"Kathy, are you the Kathy White who built this wall?"

"Yes, that's me."

Milly wiped away tears. "Kathy, you put my husband on the wall, please tell me your history. Where did you come from and how did your life get to the point of building this wonderful wall that I am looking at now."

"Milly, are you sure you want to know about my history? It goes to a dark place?"

Milly touched Kathy lightly on the arm. "I would love to hear it Kathy, I believe it was a hard journey for you."

"Yes it was, Milly. Very hard. And it still affects me to this day."

Chapter One

My full name is Kathleen White (nee Brew), I was born in Collie, Western Australia in 1950, such a long time ago.

My grandfather lived in Northam and my family owned the Ford dealership and the Brews service station. Dad was an engine driver; he drove trains until he joined the Air Force and became a navigator in World War II. After Dad was released from the Air Force, they moved to Collie. Our next move was to Wundowie, a little coal mining town, not far from Northam.

Many times throughout my life Dad would say to me, do you remember such and such from Collie? Mum would say, she was only six months old when we left Collie. Dad would always say, that was no excuse. I think he liked stirring my poor mother. Mum and Dad built a house in Cabell Street, Mt Yokine, 11 kilometres from Perth city. In those days it was the last suburb out of Perth, different now. I started to attend school at Tuart Hill and then went onto Tuart Hill High School.

I had so much trouble with learning at school, it wasn't until my brother said to me one day, I'm not surprised, "Sis, Lynette and myself, didn't have the problems you had". I looked at him a little silly, "What do you mean," I asked him. Our grandfather moved in with us when I was at school and I would come home with homework; Dad was doing shift work. If he was home, he would help me with homework and he would do it the way he had learned when he was at school. If he wasn't home, my grandfather would help me and he would do it the way he was taught at school some 80 years ago. My school teacher, also a pig farmer, kept falling asleep and would put us in charge of one of his favourite pupils for the rest of the day. It was not easy to learn under those conditions. I have struggled with reading, writing and grammar ever since.

When I left school, I started to work in an accountancy office in Perth. Well, that didn't last long, I couldn't stand being trapped within four walls and no windows.

By now my father was working as a refrigeration mechanic at the Peters Ice Cream factory in Perth. One day, a worker at this accounting firm handcuffed a suitcase to me and gave me an address with delivery instructions. It was seven blocks away and by the time I arrived there, my toes and heels were bleeding. The people at this address uncuffed the case from my wrist, then opened the case, which was full to the brim with cash notes – thousands and thousands of dollars. I started to walk back to the office but had to phone my father from a phone box on my way back to work, to ask if he would pick me up after work. It turned out, he was knocking off early that day and told me to stay where I was. When he saw my feet he went right off. He was furious when I told him I had this briefcase handcuffed to my wrist and when it was open it was full of cash notes. Dad took me back to the office and said to them, "What the hell do you think you are doing sending a 15-year-old kid to walk seven blocks, handcuffed to a case full of money". He did say a few other things and wouldn't let me go back to work there again.

I liked that idea. I found a job within walking distance from home, at a place called Freecorns, similar to the grocery shops we have today. I was put at the cash register and became very fast on it; I won a few competitions for my speed and accuracy. Of course they were the old cash registers, not like the ones they have today.

You had to stretch your fingers to hit the buttons, and you had to count the money back to the customer, as the till didn't tell you how much money to give for change.

After a year of working there, a haberdashery shop on the next corner at Mt Yokine offered me a job there. I liked that idea, so I took the job. Within one month, I became the manager.

I used to walk home from work; I started talking to a man who I saw sitting on his front steps playing the guitar. I so wanted to learn the guitar. After a few months, this man offered to teach me. I was so excited, Dad bought me a guitar. Off I went for my first lesson, then practised and practised and, as guitar players know, your fingers hurt like hell.

As I went back for my second lesson, I must admit I was starting to feel a little uncomfortable, as this house was very old, not painted, and the exterior and the garden had not been touched. Well, there was no garden, just a lot of dead shrubs. I noticed the front steps were nearly falling in and once you got inside the house it smelt very stale; the lino in the hallway was so old you couldn't work out the pattern anymore, and it was starting to roll up from the edges. The lounge chairs were so old, the fabric was tearing apart.

Why hadn't I noticed this in my first lesson, why now? I had noticed this man, named Keith, looked like he hadn't had a shower in a few months and smelt like it. This lesson, I was feeling scared, and I had no idea why. I soon found out.

I came from a family that never mentioned sex, and I had no idea what it was. As I was about to leave that afternoon, this man pinned me against his wall by my hair and took my guitar from me, he pressed his body against mine and started pumping himself against me. I told him to get off me, I tried so hard to push him off, but I was a skinny thing and he was big. I kept yelling "get off me, get off me". He kept saying "let me finish, let me finish".

Once he stepped away from me, he handed me my guitar and casually said "see you next week, keep up your practice". I flew out of there and didn't stop until I got to the corner of our street, tears flowing down my cheeks.

One of my friends, a boy I knew from school, Arnold, saw me and told me to sit down. He sat with me and asked what was wrong. I told him I was scared, and he asked why, and I told him what happened. He told me I was in danger and to never go near him again or he could end up raping me. "Oh!" I said. He said, "Kathy, do you know what rape means?" "No!" I replied. He rolled his eyes and said, "You need to talk to someone about that". I asked if he could tell me, he thought for a while and said, "Can you come to my place or do you have to go home?" I told him I could go to his place for a little while. He said he wanted me to talk to his sister or mother. I was okay with that as they were lovely people.

He went in and told them what had happened to me, and I was too scared to talk to my parents. He told them that I was scared of what my father would do to the man if he ever got a hold of him.

Arnold's sister and mother decided it would be best if I went home and talked to my mother – they felt it wasn't their place to talk to me about sex. But when I got home, I looked at my mother, who was trying to get tea, and helping my grandfather. I thought to myself, Mum has enough to deal with, I won't say anything about what this creep had done to me. Sadly, that was the start of my fear.

I was home a week later; Dad was home and asked me how the guitar was lesson going. I told him I didn't want to go again. He got very angry, that he had wasted money on a guitar, and I was tired of it so quickly. I never told my parents what happened that day; they couldn't understand why I wouldn't walk up that street, and why I quit my job.

I started to work for a drapery store at Tuart Hill called Gambanis Drapery, it was in the opposite direction to the house of horrors, as I now called it.

I looked after the shop while my boss George went in his car to the market gardens; he would sell the farming clothing from his car. I loved that job. The only problem was, a shop close to us sold the best donuts you could ever taste!

I had a great teenage life. Every weekend I would be down at Scarborough Beach, or I would be working weekends at Beatty Park swimming pool. Two places I shouldn't have been – I couldn't swim. I would spend hours trampolining because I loved that; that's the only sport I would ever do. I was hopeless with other sports, and I hated balls coming towards me.

My mother said to me one day, "Kathy you seemed to have lost your confidence since you started to play the guitar, why is that?"

I replied, "No Mum, I'm okay, it was just my fingers started to bleed, and I think I got scared. The guitar is under my bed; I'll find a good teacher one day and learn it again".

I was happy with that answer, but she knew something was wrong. I was out one night and Arnold told a few of his friends what happened to me. A few weeks later, I was told that my guitar teacher had a guitar smashed over his head and he had been beaten. I would hate to think it was because of me. I will never know, but I would never want to have anyone hurt.

Dad came home from work one night and as he was sitting at the table looking deep in thought, he suddenly said, "What do you lot think about moving to Cairns? I flew over it in the war and always wanted to go there". We said, "Yep, when are we going?"

Well, I must tell you I thought Cairns was not far from us, a little town somewhere near Perth or Northam. Did I get a reality check when I saw a map. Oh no, I have a great boyfriend and I will have to leave him, I thought. As a teenager your boyfriend is your major priority.

Me being me, I loved the idea of adventure, and a car drive that far would be the bee's knees, I thought. I told my boyfriend I could always come back. I met Max while going to marching – I used to march for the West Farmers marching team. And I had to catch the bus to Perth to practice. Max had a Harley-Davidson motorbike; he also had a car, thank goodness. My dad did not approve at all of motor bikes. But Max turned up and played cards with him one night and won him over.

When I left Western Australia, I was 18. Max's friends and over 200 bike-riding people went across the Narrows bridge with their stands down and they threw out red flames right across the bridge, across the Swan River. It was the most beautiful sight. My dear friend Jan and I were taken up to Kings park, that looks over the bridge. Some people pulled up next to us and we were all in tears. The lady said to me, "You're a lucky young lady to have friends do that for you".

My grandfather moved in with my aunt; he didn't want to travel that far. Mum and Dad cleared out the house. I have no idea what they did with it all, I just know Dad sold a Chrysler Royal for a Holden station wagon and we had a trailer full of everything we now owned, and headed across to Cairns. That drive, the grids across the Nullarbor were so high we had to crawl over them. We arrived in Sydney and stayed with my brother, who had just had his first child. I caught up with some friends from school – Sue and Ruth, who took me to see Kings Cross. What an experience that was; the first time I ever saw men dressed up like women and women dressed weird. Sue and Ruth kept saying to me, "Don't laugh, whatever you do".

When we arrived in Cairns, boy, was it hot. We stayed at a caravan park, which is now a big shopping centre.

I went to the pool with my sister to try to cool down. I am not supposed to go in pools, but it was so hot I went under the water to cool off, and as soon as I did, I thought, oh no, I shouldn't have done that. I can't go in pools because I always have ear trouble if I get water in my ears. It was starting to get late and Dad had told us to go and have a shower before we'd go and get some tea.

From the caravan park, you could see beautiful mountains, and me being me, I asked if we could go for a drive over the mountains. Well, the family nearly killed me, "Kathleen (I got Kathleen when I was in trouble), we have just driven 5,000 miles and you want to go for a drive? Go and get a shower," I was told. I thought it was a good idea. It was still daylight to go for a drive, I thought; mind you, it was getting dark.

We had a shower and then tea and decided we had better go to the toilet so we wouldn't get up through the night. Suddenly lights came on and not long after, there were two girls standing on the toilet seats, calling out, "Dad, help". As soon as the lights came on there were big beetles and butt-ugly cane toads, that we had not seen before; these creepy-looking toads came under the toilet and shower doors. They were big, a lot bigger than the ones you see these days. It was a weird place, I thought, and the doors didn't go to the floor; there was about a foot between the floor and the door, so these toads hopped under the doors. Oh! They were so ugly, one was the size of a dog I thought. Dad said, "Slight exaggeration, Kathy". Well, to me they looked like the size of a small dog.

Dad rescued us, and by 11.30 that night I was taken to the hospital, my ears were killing me; they had a cloth like a bandage dipped in thick, black gooey stuff, and they fed it through my ear. I had black gooey stuff coming out of my nose and my ear for a week. It was so embarrassing. I had what is called Tropical Ear. I wouldn't wish it on my worst enemy.

Mum and Dad were looking at houses to buy one, with me trying to hide behind everyone. They purchased a home at Aeroglen, on the side of a hill. We moved into the house, and I found a job at fashion shop Rockmans, where I met a guy named Neil. He told me his friend Garry took him to work every day, that they drove past my place and offered me a lift to and from work with them. I was happy with that as I did not like this bus-to-work idea.

I met Garry White, and we became like brother and sister; he would take me everywhere, and he introduced me to his friends. I wrote home to my friends about this different lifestyle. How everyone drinks and swears. It was weird. I didn't drink or swear or sleep around, so they thought this girl from WA was weird.

While working at Rockmans, I kept yawning daily. My manager came to me and said, "If you keep yawning, I will have to put you off – go to a doctor to find out what is causing it". I went to the doctor and he told me it was because I came from a dry heat to humidity, and it would take a while for my body to adjust.

After a few more weeks, the manager told me to go and get a blood test or lose my job. Garry and Neil told me I yawned too much.

Off I went to get this darn blood test. The doctor called me to his surgery and asked me how long I had been drinking, "Drinking!" I said, "Drinking? I have never drunk anything". He said he would have to call my parents in, that I was a wardrobe drinker. "What?" I yelled. He told me my blood test showed I had been drinking. I thought for a while and asked him if methylated spirits could be the cause of the yawning, as I had to clean the glass shelves every day with methylated spirits and every time I took the lid off the bottle, I would start to yawn even more. "Ah!" he said, "That's it". I told him I had just come off nine months of antibiotics, because I had glandular fever in WA. He said that was the answer.

From his surgery, I went straight into the ice cream shop where I used to get the yummiest hot dogs for lunch. While I was there I asked if I could get a job there, and they said I could start straight away.

I went back to the manager of Rockmans and told her it was the methylated spirits that made me yawn. She snapped at me, "What a lot of rot". I put the methylated spirits on a shelf with the rag and said, "Bye" and walked out the door.

I found out later that my Rockmans boss had tea with a doctor a few weeks later. She asked the doctor if a person could yawn from using methylated spirits every day, and he advised her not to allow the staff to use methylated spirits to clean shelves. It makes sense – methylated spirits is ethanol-based, with strong vapours.

The manager of Rockmans popped into the ice creamery to buy a hot dog one day. I nearly fell over when she apologised to me.

I was 18 when I met one of Garry's friends, Barry, and we started to go out. He would help my parents out if they were doing anything. Dad started to build a shed, he was there to help with that and with many other projects.

He kept wanting to have sex, I told him not until I was married would I do that, and I told him to leave me alone on many occasions. But he would never stop – he kept on at me to the point I was sick of it. I told my sister, and she chuckled and said that will stop when we got married.

Well, we did get married. I told my father on the way to the church that I didn't want to do this, I didn't want to get married to Barry. He just said, "Nonsense. He is a good bloke" and I was taken to the church, followed by a reception with a few people at my parents' house. I can't tell you how scared I was for that night to end; if I could have driven a car, I think I would have got in it and taken off back to Western Australia that night.

Our caravan was parked in Dad and Mum's bottom driveway. The house was on the side of a hill. In the front yard was a boulder as big as a mountain. Mum, Dad, and I dug dirt out around it to make a place to park vehicles, with steps going up to the front yard. That was where we were staying for the night. The next day we were heading to Sydney because I wanted to celebrate my 21st birthday with my brother.

On our wedding night, we went to the caravan. Remember, I had very little knowledge of this sex thing. He looked at me and literally tore my wedding dress off me and said, "You won't need that again". I must confess I was so scared; he threw me on the bed and pulled my legs apart with his fingers, his nails cut into my legs, and then he penetrated me. It was so, so, painful all I could think about was if this is sex, people live a horrid life.

I remember crying from pain, but I had to pull myself together as Mum and Dad were not far from me. At two in the morning I felt my leg being reefed to one side and my pyjamas (that he wanted me to put on) torn off, and he again penetrated me, well I was very sore now. I asked him to stop, I was in so much pain, and his reply was, "I'm married to you now, I can do what I like".

He told me to wear jeans the next morning, I figured that was so my parents couldn't see my legs. We left for Sydney the next day. I wanted to go back and pretend I had never met this guy, but I now had to go away with him. I couldn't go back.

When we arrived in Sydney, I couldn't see my brother, he was busy on my birthday. Barry insisted we leave Sydney and go to Mackay. I was disappointed, I just wanted to visit my brother for my birthday but missed out. I don't think my brother even knew it was my 21st birthday.

Barry didn't like Mackay, so after a few weeks we headed back to Cairns. He went back to painting houses; he was a painter and decorator.

I was offered a job, window decorating for retailer David Jones. I so wanted that job, but Barry told me I couldn't take it. I had no idea why he was against me working as a window dresser. I had a feeling it was because they said they would send me to Brisbane, and Sydney for training.

I worked at Tovey's chemist for a while and when I didn't turn up for work, one of the girls came to see why I didn't go back. I was in the caravan in tears, and I told her I couldn't go back but I couldn't tell her why – I just asked her to understand. After she left I just cried for three hours. I was sore from head to toe, bruised and so embarrassed and confused as to why was I having problems with this sex thing; no one else was walking around bruised and sore and if they were, they were hiding it well. I couldn't understand how women had smiles on their faces. Was something wrong with me? Why were they smiling? This sex is painful.

Barry would put his hand down my top and grab my breast squeeze it and twist it at the same time. Many times he made my breast bleed and left me with huge bruises.

He loved doing it when my periods were due because I was so sore, and he would grab my breast squeeze it and I would very quietly scream in pain. Because we were living in a caravan park, I couldn't squeal as loud as I would have liked.

He decided to go and live at Redcliffe because his brother was living there. I think he wanted to take me away from my parents.

I told Barry to sell the caravan. I wasn't going to live in it anymore, I threatened to leave him and go back to my parents if he didn't sell it. To this day, I don't know why I didn't, but in my heart, I didn't want to upset my parents. We rented a house at Scarborough Beach on the Redcliffe Peninsula, further down the coast, close to Brisbane.

My parents moved to Karumba in the Gulf country after we left Cairns. One year, they came to stay with us for a holiday and while they were with us, they decided to buy a home in a quiet street in the suburb of Margate on the Redcliffe Peninsula.

They asked us to move into their house until they moved down from Karumba. We moved into their home for them. I was sad because I liked living on the waterfront at Scarborough. I was pregnant with our daughter at the time.

When Mum and Dad came down to live, we lived together for a short time, and I was glad because it quietened Barry down, a lot.

Dad and Barry had decided it would be best for us to have a place of our own. I was happy living with my parents because Barry would be as nice as pie around my father. But there is always a but, it was too late for me to protest. Dad had loaned Barry $10,000 for a deposit on a house in Dunbar Street, Margate, only three streets from their home. In my heart, I knew I couldn't stay with my parents, that wouldn't be fair on them.

Oh, being pregnant with someone like Barry was no thrill. When I had our daughter, the nurses got so angry with me when I couldn't breastfeed her that they had me in tears. I told them to leave me alone as politely as I could, but they still got angry with me. My doctor walked past the room and saw me in tears and came in and asked me what was wrong with me. I told him what Barry did to my breasts, including through my pregnancy. I told him my nipples were red and split. He asked if he could have a look. I told him, not without a nurse being present. He agreed and then left instructions for the nursing staff to leave me alone. From then on they were very supportive.

Barry came to pick us up from the hospital. Our daughter had the most beautiful silver coloured hair, everyone commented on it. I wanted to go home, but no, Barry took us to Chermside shopping centre. I was exhausted. He bought me a ring and a coat even after I told him I didn't want anything and asked to go home. "No," he said.

At the shopping centre, we ran into some of his work friends. They said how gorgeous our baby was with that silver hair. Barry said, "Yes, she is going to be a prostitute, and I will live off her earnings". I hit his arm and said, "Don't say that – that's a horrid thing to say about your daughter". His blunt reply was, "Why not, that's what I'll do". I saw the expression on the faces of these people. They looked at me, and by then I was about to collapse. One couple said, "Come with me Kathy, come and sit at this café, we'll get you a cuppa". I thanked them and one asked when I got out of hospital. I told them I just got out and I was tired and sore, as I had eight stitches.

Barry returned from getting a drink and said, "Eight stitches, I didn't realise that". One of his mates said to him, "What sort of a husband are you?" He just looked at him with a smirk on his face.

We had a cuppa and thankfully headed home. I fed our daughter and put her back to sleep, she was a good baby.

I wanted to go and lie down for a while. I started to go to sleep, the next thing I knew, my dress was pulled up, my undies pulled off me, and I was forced on my back and raped with stitches in. He told me he wanted to know what it would be like to have sex with stitches in. I have never been so sore in my life. I had to go to the doctor the next day. I walked there, though Barry had told me not to go near the doctor.

The doctor was horrified by what I went through, fixed me up and had to put me back on penicillin in case I got an infection. He told me to tell my husband to leave me alone, I had just had a baby. The doctor told me to tell Barry he wants to talk with him, as soon as possible.

Well! That was like talking to a brick wall.

Barry told me "You can do anything to a woman, and it won't hurt her".

He would take us for a drive on the weekend over the border to New South Wales; we had to sit in the car while he went and bought porno magazines.

I told him if he ever put those horrid magazines anywhere I could see them, I would burn the house down.

One cold windy day, Barry huffed at me and went downstairs

for a few moments. A while later, Barry entered our bedroom, grabbed my hair, threw me on the bed and pulled me to a sitting position, then stood beside me with a handgun. He placed the gun at my temple on the right side of my head and said, "I have a bullet in there somewhere, let me see if we can find it before I rape the s**t out of you, I prefer not to have your brains laying all over the room though". I heard the gun click on his first try to find a bullet. He laughed, "Are you still here?" he asked.

Then he clicked the gun once more. Our daughter was awake and starting to whimper a little. "She had better shut up or she will get the next bullet," he said.

I won't go on about this, except to say he threw the handgun on the floor and grabbed my hair and pulled me into our daughter's room and threw me on the floor and raped me in front of her. He then left the house, and yes, the gun was loaded, and the bullet was in the next chamber. Luckily our daughter had gone back to sleep and didn't see anything that happened.

The other part of this story is almost the same scenario only this time it was a very thin, sharp knife at my throat, and I could feel the blood running slowly down my neck from a small point of the blade that dug into my neck.

These two incidents have triggered stress in me on many occasions.

One day I became sick and had to find my way to the doctor. He told me I had an infection and put me back on penicillin. I told him I suffered thrush with penicillin, and he told me it was the only thing that would fix my infection.

The thrush set in; Barry wouldn't leave me alone. I was red raw and bleeding from the thrush, but he didn't care at all. He came home one afternoon at about three o'clock, I had our daughter in the high chair, and I was cooking something on the stove, and I didn't hear him come in. Having his own painting business, he could come home any time he liked.

I was standing over the stove when he came in from behind me and yanked my shorts and underpants down in one move. I burnt my hands and screamed, I remember yelling at him for the first time, "Touch me again and I'll put this fry pan over your head". I took off and out the door I went. Would you believe I had to take two dogs back home because they started to follow me along the way.

I started to walk over to my parents' house; they had now moved to West End. Off I went, sore from thrush, red raw and bleeding, with my hands now stinging from the burns. I had no money, and I was going to walk from Redcliffe to West End, 40 kilometres away. The anger kept me going, I had no idea where I was when a taxi driver stopped and asked if I was okay. I told her I wasn't, and I didn't know what to do. She told me she had seen me a few times while taking her passengers to and fro, and that she would be happy to take me to my parents' home.

I arrived at my parents' place and they were worried sick. They insisted on paying the taxi lady, who told them they didn't have to, but Dad insisted before she wished me all the best and left.

I thought great, now I can tell my parents what was going on. But no! Barry had called them and told them the thrush was getting to me, and I took off to go and see them. He told them he was worried sick; he thought I had burnt myself on the stove. He told them he had to stay there with our daughter, and would they look after me, and bring me home.

Well, that put me right back to not being able to tell them exactly what happened.

When people later asked why I stayed with him so long, I explained that he kept reminding me my parents would lose their money for the house deposit if I left or told anyone. At that time, I believed what I was experiencing was typical in a marriage. Even when I sought assistance from the police, I was informed that they couldn't intervene because I was married.

I went back to the doctor the next day for help, but I knew while Barry still wanted his sex, I would never recover from this thrush. The creams were not helping. The doctor asked when my husband going to see him. I told him, "He reckons you can do anything to a woman, and you can't hurt them". The doctor was not impressed.

One morning I had a dreadful migraine and the doctor came and gave me two needles – one to help me sleep and one to stop the vomiting; Mum and Dad had come over to help me.

The doctor had given me the injections and left before Barry turned up, and Mum and Dad said, "Now you're home we will head off, Kathy needs rest". I was trying to scream, *no don't go…* but I couldn't, they left, and all I can remember was Barry jumping on my chest and assaulting me. We had a water bed, he dropped on my chest and the water come up under me, damaging my lungs. I ended up in the hospital for a while.

The day I was to be released from the hospital, I asked the doctor to let me stay in but he told me he couldn't, sorry, before asking me how I got so much damage. My reply to him was, "You're sending me home to get more".

He held my hand and said, "Can I suggest you go to the police and ask for help".

I thought *what a good idea, I'll do that.* I went home the next day and walked to the police station (it wasn't too far away).

The very kind policeman told me they couldn't do anything because I was married to him, and they couldn't interfere with marriages.

By now I thought if anyone else suggested I go to the police, I'd scream at them.

I had no friends anymore. No one wanted to come to our

place because in front of people, Barry would put his hand down my top and twist my breast in front of people. It was sickening.

He had me on the floor one day. I had bought a pair of very tight jeans and a belt and a skivvy that wrapped tight around my neck with long sleeves; I thought that would stop him.

One day he grabbed the collar of my top and pulled it as hard as he could, shoved his hand down my bra and twisted my breast until the nipple bleed and said, "Nothing will stop me doing what I enjoy".

My neighbours used to say to me, "Kathy, why are you wearing jeans and polo-neck tops in the middle of summer? We're hot just looking at you". I would reply, "The heat doesn't worry me at all". I didn't want them to see the bruises I had from my neck to my knees.

Barry got a vasectomy after we had our daughter – he said he didn't want more kids if I was going to get thrush again, that it made it uncomfortable for him. Years later he told me it was my fault he had the vasectomy. I guess that was because I had the thrush so bad.

I was down at the shop one day, when I came home and walked into the house, on the floor were pornographic magazines, open with vulgar pictures.

Words cannot describe my anger, my fear. If my father hadn't put up the deposit for the house I think I would have followed through with my threat and burnt the house down, but I had my daughter to think about as well as my dad and neighbours, and I didn't want their houses to catch fire.

From that day on I was trying so hard to work out how the hell I was going to get out of this. My daughter's safety was my priority. A week later I was at a park and my daughter slipped and fell from a bench seat that had slats across it – her foot became caught in the back seat, and her shin went over the front.

I told Barry we had to take her to get her leg checked. He said, "No, I'll fix her up". I told him it was probably broken. He still said no.

The next day I said I was taking her to the doctor, and he told me if I did, he'd chain me to a post and "rape the s**t" out of me.

I didn't care. By now her leg was more important to me than anything.

I carried her to a doctor, then onto X-rays after banging the doctor's desk and telling him I wanted her leg X-rayed. The radiographers told me not to move her; her leg was snapped. Off we went to get it plastered.

When Barry came home he was furious with me and lifted his hand to me. I stood there and said in the firmest voice I could, said, "Go ahead, hit me. When you're asleep I will get a lump of three by two and bash you over the head – you will never hit me again". I must have shocked him; he pulled back and walked out the door.

About two weeks later I was sitting on the edge of the bed, rolling up a bandage. Barry was sitting beside me wrapping up another one, as his apprentice had hurt himself and I had used the bandages on him.

I spotted a little bug on the side of Barry's face and lightly hit at it. He raised his hand and slapped me on the face, I held my face and said, "Why did you do that?" He said I hit him first. I told him I was flicking off a bug, I didn't want to squash it on his face, so I flicked it off. My face was so red, he got up and left the house, as he had a habit of doing.

I thought *that's it, I will not live with someone who hits me*. I still thought what I was going through with the sex thing was normal in marriages, and that every other person was going through the same as me. I thought that was what being married was about. I could not understand why people had smiles on their faces and held hands and cuddled each other in public. He held my hand when we went out, but my hand used to get so sore. He must have thought I was going to escape his grip and run. I didn't want him touching me.

I eventually formed a friendship with a woman named Jenny, who I met when our children began kindergarten together. I would invite Jenny to our home, on occasions when I was aware that Barry was working on the other side of Brisbane, ensuring he wouldn't return unexpectedly. Although I hadn't disclosed the situation to her, we developed a strong relationship that continues to this day. Despite going our separate ways, we have remained friends.

I was trying everything I could to work out how to get out of this marriage.

One morning, the phone rang, and it was a lady we knew from Cairns, who our old friend Garry considered a mother figure. She had found us in the phone book; it turned out that she lived only a few streets away. She informed me that there was someone with her who would love to see us – Garry.

Garry was down from Cairns and wanted to come and visit us. I said yes straight away, I hadn't seen Garry for over seven years, and as I said, Garry was like a brother to me, he had married and moved to Karumba, the last I had heard.

I phoned Barry at his workplace. I knew there was no way I could have Garry at the house without him being home. Just as Barry pulled up at the house, so did Garry in a truck.

It didn't take long for me to realise Barry wasn't coming near me while Garry was there. I felt like I could breathe for once, when someone was in the house.

Garry told us he was divorced and had twin boys, but he didn't get to see them. He told Barry he was going to be carting grain and was looking for somewhere to stay down here for a while. To my amazement, Barry said he could stay with us.

Garry only came home every now and then. He would have his clothes and truck bedding washed, and have a feed and be gone again. Sometimes he slept over, but not often; I had to make sure Barry was home every time he came. I must admit I loved it when Garry was there, Barry never came near me. I felt like I couldn't take any more pain.

I was scared when Barry built a room under the house for the laundry. He had a lock on it, with space for a big padlock. I said, "This laundry is a bit big, isn't it?" "No!" he said, "it's big enough for a bed". I thought he was going to put Garry down there, but no, he said it was for our daughter when she would get a little older. "When she misbehaves, I will lock her in there and I will come down, wriggle the handle and ask her if she will behave – I'll do that a few times before I open the door and put a leather strap around her bum". I froze, "Like hell you will," I said, and grabbed the padlock and threw it in a bin. He went and pulled the padlock out of the bin and looked at me angrily as I walked back upstairs. I was glad to see Garry come in for tea and sleep, because I knew what was going to happen to me if he hadn't come.

The next day Garry said he was going to Cairns and I asked if I could go with him; I told him I wanted to go and see my sister. He said of course I could go. I told Barry I was going to Cairns with Garry to see my sister. He said, "You don't get on with your sister," I said, "I do, we just haven't seen each other, and I want to visit her and I'm going whether you like it or not".

The next day, when Garry and I were about to leave, I was standing on the top step of our high-set house, and Garry was at the bottom step. Barry kept asking me if he could touch my boobs before I go. No goodbye or anything, just "Can I touch your boobs before you go?" I couldn't believe it.

I did go. I told him he could look after our daughter, and I said she was his daughter too.

We headed out and as we reached Deception Bay turn off, only 12 kilometres from home, it was just starting to get dark, when Garry said, "What does this wanker want?" I said, "Who?" and he replied, "Barry, he is coming up beside me". "What?" I said.

Garry pulled over and Barry jumped on the sidestep of the truck to Garry's window and gave him his shaving bag, "You left this behind," he said.

I looked in the car – a station wagon – and asked, "Where's our girl? Who is looking after her?" "She's home in bed, she went to sleep," he replied as he leapt off the truck steps and drove away.

"Asleep?"

We had only left the house 30 minutes earlier. She was only five years old, and was left in the house on her own. I put my hand over my mouth to try to stop crying.

I asked Garry why he called Barry a wanker, as I thought they were great friends.

"Kathy, I'm not blind, I can see he gives you hell by your actions – you jump every time he walks into the room. You wear clothes that I can tell you are hiding something. It's not my business but I want you to know, if you need help, I'm all ears." Well! that was my breaking point, I had the biggest meltdown you could ever imagine. Our daughter was left home at night in a wooden home. I knew that a lady who lived not far from us left her three kids asleep to go and get some milk one night and her house burnt down with the kids inside. I was devastated. *What have I done? I have left her with him.*

I pulled myself together and tried not to think of the worst but it had hit me more than I thought and I started vomiting, from Deception Bay to Cairns. Every time Garry stopped at a service station I would end up in the toilets, vomiting; he even had to pull up on the side of the road a few times so I could be sick. That was not easy in a fully loaded truck. I felt so sorry for Garry, but he was so understanding. He told me he could see something was wrong between Barry and me, but he didn't think it was his place to say anything to me.

I talked and he listened, and when we arrived in Cairns the next day he took me straight to a doctor; he was worried I was dehydrating.

The doctor said to me, "What is wrong?" I replied, "I have been vomiting from Deception Bay to here". "Yes, I know that, but what is wrong," he said. I thought, *stupid bloody doctor, I'm sick*. He looked at me with very kind eyes and said, "Something very, very deep brought this vomiting on. Are you going to tell me what?" I blurted out a little about what was going on at home.

He said he wanted to talk to Garry. I said no, he had nothing to do with it. He brought me to see my sister, but she wasn't home. Garry had to return south, so I also needed to go back with Garry to have a way to get home or I might be stranded, and I didn't know where my sister was (we didn't have mobile phones then). "I need to talk to her," I said.

The doctor insisted on talking to Garry. I felt like a fool, standing in front of his door trying to stop him from calling Garry into his room. The doctor lifted me up under my arms, and put me to one side, and said, "Come in, Garry". He told Garry to please make sure he took me to my parents' house before he took me home, that's all he said to him. Garry said he would do that.

On our arrival back at West End, I told my parents I was leaving Barry. I explained a little of why I was leaving him. Dad said Barry needed help. Garry, and my parents thought it would be best if I went home and told Barry in person that I was leaving him. Dad promised to be there first thing in the morning to pick me up.

We arrived back at Redcliffe from West End, Barry stepped up on my side of the truck and my instincts locked the truck door. I realised what I had done and unlocked it and got out. His first words were, "I got you a gift – it's on the bed". I thought straight away, I bet I know what it is. We went upstairs. Garry said he was going to have a shower. I went into the bedroom to put my bag down. I was lucky Barry had taken our daughter to my parents' house for the weekend. I asked Mum and Dad to keep her with them for me.

Sure enough, sitting on the bed was a pair of undies and a bra with the crutch and nipples missing out of them.

I walked back into the kitchen, Barry looked at me and said, "Are you leaving me?" I said, "Yes, but you have to go and get help. The doctor wants to have a talk with you – I told you that before. I will come back if you get that help".

Our bathroom was beside the kitchen. Garry heard this, had tea and left; he had to go and get the truck loaded.

Well, what a night that was. He didn't ask why or where I was going, what about our daughter, nothing. His words to me the whole night, and I mean the entire night, was, wait for it, "Can I have sex before you leave?"

By 4 am I wanted to mutilate him. Luckily my parents turned up to pick me up at 6.30am as they were worried.

Barry didn't ask any questions; I found that strange. He told Dad to look after me. I told Dad it was weird that he didn't even ask if I was running off with Garry, or about our daughter or where I was going, and I didn't tell Dad that all he wanted was sex before I left.

Dad didn't say anything. I had told Mum and Dad that I was leaving him, but if he got help I would go back to him. Dad was happy with that, he was one of those men who had this thing that if you are married, you are married.

We arrived at my parents' house. Two hours later Barry turned up. He gave me a bag I had left behind; it was a bag I didn't want, and he just used it as an excuse to come over. He gave it to Dad and then left without a word.

That night he called, and I told him if he went to get some help, I would return. His reply was, "I have cancer". That was interesting, I thought. When I asked, "What doctor told you that?" I got no reply. Okay, I said, "Well book yourself into our doctor – he told me to send you to him".

"No, not doing that," was his reply. "Okay," I said and "bye".

I went to have a shower and said to Mum, "Darn, I meant to ask Barry for $10 to buy our daughter some new school shoes". She had only just started grade one and the shoes I bought for her were cutting into the back of her heels.

The phone rang again, "Barry," I said, "I need $10 to buy our girl some new school shoes". His reply was, "Well guess what, you're not getting $10, she can suffer with you". My reply was, "Well then if that's your attitude towards your own daughter, I'm getting a divorce".

I had my shower and put on a pair of pyjamas that I had made at school but had not worn before. The bottoms were like underpants. I stood between Mum and Dad's chairs. Mum looked across towards Dad and screamed, "My god what has happened to you?"

Dad looked across at Mum and said "WHAT THE HELL?" You see, as they looked across at each other they couldn't miss seeing my very purple, going yellow bruises from Barry digging his fingers and nails into my upper legs. I was bruised from my knees to my buttocks and breasts.

They were devastated, but Dad said, "He needs help. Once he gets help, you'll be safe to go back to him".

About a week later I asked Mum if Garry could stay with them until he headed back up north. I told Garry he could stay with Barry, but he refused to go back and stay with Barry but would stay in his truck at some service station. Mum and Dad were only too happy for him to stay there, as they knew him.

A week later I went over to the house at Margate to collect

some of our daughter's stuff. I wanted a writing desk that we bought for our daughter so she could do her homework. When I arrived, all our clothes were thrown out the windows on the ground. There was one note, 'you're not having that desk!'. Okay, I thought, I went through what I wanted and picked up a bank book. I looked up at the house and had to laugh – there were three-inch nails in front of the locks on the house and on the casement windows; it looked ridiculous. That was because he had taught me how to break into homes if owners forgot to leave a key when we had to paint their houses. In those days there was no house I couldn't get into, hence the three-inch nails to stop me from getting into the house. I laughed and handed the bank book to Dad and said, give this to Barry, there is enough money in there to pay a house payment.

Three days later Dad handed the bank book back to Barry, but Barry said, "No, Phil you give it to Kathy, she will need it". Well, Dad thought that was wonderful of him and told me to have patience. He said he was going to get help.

The next day, Dad drove me to the bank at Redcliffe, to get the money out. I went to the teller, she said, "Sorry, Kathy, Barry came in yesterday afternoon and closed that bank account".

I went out of the bank and walked past Dad's door, threw the bank book in his window and said, "He closed the account yesterday afternoon". Well! That bank book flew straight back out the window with Dad saying, "Get back in there and tell them that's your money". I loved Dad dearly but gee when he spoke, I jumped. I walked back into the bank and stood there, trying to work out what I could do.

The manager knew me and asked if he could help. I asked him if we could go into his office, and off we went. I explained a little bit about my situation, and he went to the files. In those days you did everything at the bank on little cards. He asked me who filled in this card to open the bank account. I said "I did". "Good," he replied, "Write the word 'separate' here," pointing to a blank space on the card. I did that and he went to the counter and gave me the funds, of $365. I thanked him, and the girl behind the counter glared at me, so I smiled at her and waved the money in front of her as I walked out.

I got in the back seat of Dad's car, and my father's hands were on the steering wheel so tight his fingers had gone white. I had never heard my father swear before but he said to me "If you ever go near that bastard again, I will belt you," I knew he didn't mean that, but I now knew that it took money, not bruises, for Dad to see what type of man he was. Mum told me he couldn't comprehend how any man would do that to a woman, let alone his daughter. So, he buried his head in the sand, but the money side of it made him see what an asshole Barry was.

Our daughter had started a school at West End. I had a flat across the road from Mum and Dad. Garry stayed with Mum and Dad and would visit me when he returned to Brisbane.

I was worried about how I was going to make a living; I was now terrified to go out on my own. I still am, to this day. You see, one day Barry tied me to the bed and put a blindfold on my eyes. He told me he had his mates coming over, and they were going to have sex with me so he could watch. Oh my gosh, I tore the skin of my wrists and ankles trying to get out of there. I heard two men's voices and panicked, one said, "Mate, this is your wife, isn't it?" "Yep," he said. "But don't worry about that, she will be okay." I fought those restraints.

The second man said, "Go to hell, Barry, you're a shit of a man to do that to your wife or any woman," and they both left. Barry was furious and left me tied up for the rest of the day. As usual, he left the house.

To this day I am so scared one of these men is going to walk up to me and say, "I remember you". Hence my fear.

After that incident I had gone back to the police twice more to ask for help but was given the same answer, "You're married, we can't do anything".

Barry said to me constantly, "You're married to me, I can do whatever I like to you". And he used to tell other men that "You can do anything to a woman, and you can't hurt her".

One day when I was out grocery shopping with Mum and Dad, at West End we arrived at the end of the checkout, about to walk away, and a voice said, "Hi Kathy". I nearly died – it was a detective whose house Barry had painted, at West End. Back then, I had helped Barry paint inside the cupboards at the detective's house. "I hear you have left Barry." My heart sank; I thought he was going to tell me off or something. "It's about time you left that asshole. Can I give you a hug and tell you I am sorry I could never help you?" I asked him how he knew there was a problem. He told me he noticed that every time Barry was painting his house, when he walked in the room where I was, I would jump. "I even saw you three times hide in our pantry and the broom cupboard until he left the room. I used to see you shake." All I could say to the detective was "Oh". But you know what, to hear that from that detective that day at that shop check out and to receive that hug, was the best thing that could have happened to me at that time of my life.

After a few months, Garry and I became very close. His grandmother was ill in Cairns and he wanted to go up to her. He asked me if I would go with him, and he told me he would look after me and my daughter. That's when our friendship grew to a relationship, but I did feel sorry for Garry – I had so much fear in me that it took quite a few years for me to relax and realise, I was safe with him now.

After his grandmother passed away we moved up to Mareeba

in far north Queensland and lived in a converted tobacco shed outside the town; we were there for a few years.

I eventually learned not all men were like Barry. I knew I was safe with Garry, but I still had years of baggage I had to work through. I ended up pregnant and could only carry my second-born, Dionne, for six months. They had to take her from me as the internal damage I had suffered from Barry's constant abuse had left more injuries than I realised – the placenta stopped feeding her and my body wasn't strong enough to carry a baby. When she was born, I died. I collapsed in the toilets and lost so much blood. She was born weighing three pounds eight ounces (or just over 1.5kg). Ten days later I saw her for the first time, and we were allowed to go home a week later.

Out of the blue and just after I gave birth to Dionne, I received a letter from a solicitor telling me I had to hand my first-born daughter, now aged seven, over to Barry for the weekend. This was on the Monday.

Apparently he had re-married and told me he couldn't have kids, so he wanted our daughter, because I had another girl. Well, that was a joke, he hadn't come near his daughter for two years. To receive a letter from this solicitor telling me, I had to hand her over to him and his wife that weekend, for the weekend? I had no idea who this wife was.

Long story short, I went to a solicitor, and he couldn't have her; he had to take me to court to see her. I had a court order dictating that the only access he could have with her was with my parents at West End – and that court order was for Brisbane and now we all lived in Cairns. The solicitor told me he would have to go back to court to have that changed to Cairns.

I agreed to go to a mediator. I believed that he could see her, being her father, so I suggested we meet at a beach a few weeks in a row, and have a picnic lunch together. That way, she could get to know them both. It was agreed. The mediator told me she wished more people were understanding, like me. I didn't have the heart to tell her that I was boiling inside.

When it was time to decide which beach would work best, Barry walked in the door, arms crossed, and said, "I want nothing to do with any of this – me and my wife are going around Australia". We never saw him again, and he never paid the $10 a week to help support her.

CHAPTER TWO

Over the years I went on many trips with Garry and soon realised so many truck drivers have terrible truck accidents and are left with disabilities or are killed.

I used to say to Garry that someone needs to build a truck drivers' memorial.

When considering setting one up, I was told by a rather nasty person, that I had nothing to do with trucks and didn't know about them. Well, I think after 46 years involved with trucks, owning our own company, I figured I should know something.

When I was 12 years old living in Mt Yokine, Western Australia, I had a friend named Stephanie who lived directly behind our house. Her father was a truck driver. I used to go to her house and we would help her father wash the truck. I thought they were the best days of my life.

Mr Stewart's regular run was from Perth to the Pilbara every week. On this special week when he returned he presented me with a rock from the Pilbara. It's beautiful, with a very deep red colour on top of it, and looks like two brown eggs, a bit hard to explain. Would you believe, after 62 years, I still have that rock, and it means the world to me. Mr Stewart would tell me about his travels and things that would happen to him.

I went home one day and told my father I was going to be a truck driver. Well, he nearly spat his tea in his mouth across the table; my mother froze in the kitchen, and a little grunt left her lips as I turned to the fridge.

Dad's reply was, "My daughter will not drive trucks". End of that conversation; I was never game enough to mention that again.

Years later with my first husband Barry, we owned a truck and we used to go and pick up bags of chicken, cow, and horse manure around the Redcliffe area and deliver it to people's houses for their gardens. That was a hard job — those bags were smelly and dusty and what was worse was that we had to go to the stables, chook runs, and dairy farms and shovel it into bags then deliver it. A hard, smelly job.

On our way home one day a motorbike driver came around a corner too fast and went under our truck. It was the worst feeling I have ever felt, to see a human disappear under your wheels — so sickening. Luckily he survived.

After my divorce about four years after I left Barry, I married Garry, who was a long-distance truck driver. *Welcome to the world of trucks*, I thought. I went with Garry as many times as I could over the years. Some of the things that happened on some of the trips we went on were amazing, scary, and heartbreaking.

On one trip we went from Cairns to Karumba (an eight-hour drive by car) and arrived at Karumba on New Year's Eve; we had to go on a barge to Aurukun (usually a 12-hour drive by car). The roads were too wet to take aviation fuel in by road. Garry backed the trailer on the barge after removing the mudguards from the drive, and the legs from under the trailer, spare tyres and brackets holding them. This had to be done to allow the truck to go up on the barge. Just as we finished there was a yell of "Happy New Year".

We set sail, straight into a cyclone. Well, guess who spent the whole way up to Aurukun in a bed, vomiting constantly; you guessed it, me. I was so seasick and what didn't help was that I'm terrified of water — I couldn't swim. What was I doing on a barge in a cyclone? We arrived at Aurukun and a team had to use a dozer and a grader to pull the Kenworth truck called 'Pegasus' across the beach – that's the only place the barge could access.

I was trying to get photos of the truck coming off, and some children from the Indigenous mission turned up on the beach. I was trying to take a photo of the truck coming off the barge and the children kept jumping up and down in front of the camera, so I turned away from the barge to the beach behind me, and they followed the camera. I quickly turned back to the truck. I managed to get one photo in before the kids were in front of the camera once more. The kids just kept getting in front of the camera.

It wasn't long before the dozer and grader brought the truck back and we set sail once more. I waved to the kids; thank heavens my sea sickness had disappeared.

The next time we went back to Aurukun was by road. We turned off the highway onto the muddy dirt road and suddenly we were up to the axles in mud. We dug mud out, but it would rain again, and more mud would wash back into where we had dug out the mud before. We were exhausted at one stage and Garry said, "Strip, and we will soap up and catch this rain that is coming, to wash off the soap". "Strip, I'm not stripping, anyone could see me, I'll keep my pants and T- shirt on, thank you," I said.

Well, would you believe the rain went across us alright, at the front of the truck and the end of the trailer, but not in the middle where we were standing, waiting to have the rain wash the soap from us? Garry filled up buckets of water and he threw that over us.

All dried and sitting in the cab of the truck for a short rest, I said to Garry, "What is this, coming?" A Toyota driver came flying up to the front of the truck before reversing as fast as he could, driving beside us before getting stuck on a log. The driver then reversed back and forward until he came clear of the log, and took off. I looked at Garry and said, "No one will see us, you said". He laughed and said, "That's a grog runner – he won't stop for anyone

– he's on his way to pick up illegal alcohol to take back to the mission, as it's a dry mission and you can't take alcohol in there". "Will he get us some help," I asked. "No, he won't care about us, he just wants that grog." The Toyota came back, got stuck on the same log, and then kept going.

We dug mud out from under the wheels of the truck for hours. I would find branches of trees to put in the holes, and as quick as we would bail out the water, more would seep in. It felt like we were never going to get out of this; I was glad we only had one trailer on that trip. I would ask if we could make a cuppa – anything to get out of digging, as my hands had blisters on them. I was so grateful when Garry would say "let's have a break". We would make some lunch, have a rest for a while, then get back to more digging. The rain would come again; we were too wet to get in the truck, so we kept finding branches to push under the wheels. When I was too exhausted to keep going, Garry would tell me to wash up and jump in the cab and have a rest. But I couldn't leave him working on his own. The mud was smelling like pigs had been wallowing in it. Garry said it was just that area – the soil was very muddy. We had our supplies of food and drink with us. Garry was used to getting bogged in these areas; I always knew when he was late to arrive home from his trips up to the top end of Queensland that he was probably bogged somewhere. After a few days I would call the company we subcontracted for and check to see if they knew anything about his whereabouts, and they mostly kept me informed of any problems. Two days later, a dozer turned up to get us out. The firm we were carting for suddenly realised the truck was missing.

On another trip, Garry was helping a man called Charlie from outback Normanton who owned cattle trucks. There were three triple road train cattle trucks and when we came to a small hill, the trucks stopped at its base; I wondered why.

The next thing, they each used a stiff bar to hook up the trucks together so one truck could pull them over the hill, and the last truck would push them. It was amazing to be in the truck and look in the rearview mirror to see nine trailers and two prime movers working together.

On our way out after loading, we had to hook up again. Once the trucks were loaded with cattle, I could see why they had to use the stiff bars to get over that, what I thought was a little, hill. What is a stiff bar, some people might be asking. It's a very heavy, quite thick, hunk of metal with two round holes at each end – they hook them into the ring feeder and bull bar of trucks, to hook them together for jobs like this. It was amazing to be in the truck to experience this; we were taking these cattle from Mt Surprise to Bluff Downs station, 1,200 km from Brisbane.

In front of us was a truck with a load of cattle; it rolled on a corner. It was a horrific site, I won't go into detail, but it left me upset for weeks later.

We moved from Mareeba to Holloways Beach in Cairns while we were waiting for our house to be built in Edmonton, also in Cairns, on a block of land Garry owned. My parents had moved up to Atherton and my sister was in Cairns, so I felt at home. But one day as Mum and Dad and I were walking down the street, who should come out of a driveway in front of us, Barry. My world dropped, as I thought he was still living down south. I kept walking. He spoke to Dad and he didn't even ask anything about our daughter. He just told Dad he was selling the house, and the deposit would go back into his bank account – apparently he had a tax bill so high he had to sell, he told Dad. I still, after all these years, cannot work out how he sold that house without my signature on the papers.

Chapter Three

Our house was finished being built in Edmonton and we moved in, and Dad came down from Atherton and helped us build a large shed in the backyard.

After a few years, Garry started to say he wanted to get out of trucks. He came home one day and asked if I would like to go and live at Normanton – we had been offered a job out there in a café. Me being the adventurous type, jumped at it. We had started a little video business, and the videos were in this café; the owner hired them out for us. Garry would deliver the tapes to her.

We moved to a room at the back of the café and worked there for a while. But I didn't like café work. My kids were my priority, and if my kids were ill, I stayed with them. The owner wasn't happy with that idea. My eldest daughter was now aged 11. The youngest was five. Both girls had settled in quite well to the move. They had developed different personalities. My eldest loved horses, so we encouraged her along this path. As for Dionne, being born premature didn't deter her – she was very lively and wanted to know how everything worked. Even if an ant walked across a piece of grass, she wanted to know why the grass didn't fall over.

I went to the Aboriginal community centre and asked about an empty house. At first they didn't want to give it to me, but in the end they agreed with me – I told them they would be better off getting rent than leaving the house standing there, empty. We set the whole front of the house up with rows and rows of videos in the lounge and blocked off the rest of the house with a cupboard. We had a little desk at the front door to take the money etc; we hired video machines and TVs as well as videos.

We worked out of there for a few years, until we built a shop and a house opposite the Normanton railway. We bought two blocks of land for $5,000 in 1986.

Normanton is just south of the Gulf of Carpentaria. Its population hovers around 1,000 or so people, to give you a picture of the smallish community we lived in.

Living in isolation, like we were, we had to rely on trucks to bring us, and the town everything we needed. Our best man at our wedding, David, brought us supplies – to build our house, and shops (they were being built beside each other) – on the back of his road train. We only had one week in Cairns to buy what we needed. I mean, everything, from the foundations to the roof. It was too far to go to the store to pick anything up if we forgot something. We had a list of items we needed from the builder and the house plans with us.

I remember having an argument with the carpet layer in Cairns. I wanted the black imitation slate lino in the kitchen and dining room. He told me I needed white. I said, "But the walls are grey with white trimmings", and he eventually decided he would bring the lino himself as he'd wanted to visit Normanton, "And I'll bring the black and the white". I won the argument – black it was.

We now owned a video store and a delicatessen we called Your Choice Video and Delicatesson. I spelt it Delicatesson – I thought that would make people look, and they did. Tourists came in to comment on it and buy a coffee or tea or sweets. My miss-spelling on purpose, worked.

Of course, my husband being a truck driver for many years, was supposed to take on the video store to get out of trucks. As we know, trucking is in the blood. He used to help some station owners to drive their trucks. He also drove trucks occasionally for Charlie, the local cattle carter.

I worked in our shops daily and was lucky to have some great staff. This allowed me to go on trips with Garry now and then. I loved the trucks as well, that was my biggest downfall. Once you've been in them, driving over the vast country of ours, it's so hard to get out of them. Garry used to call me 'Blue' – he said I was like a cattle dog. Open the door of the truck and I would jump in.

When the wet season arrives, you are isolated. We learned to stock up on supplies. In those days, trucks didn't come through the wet season. That could last anywhere, from a few weeks to months sometimes.

Over time living in Normanton, we would hear of the deaths in truck accidents of some of our mates we had met in many parts of Australia including on the Bruce, Hume, Peninsula and Savannah highways during trucking runs. We lived too far away to attend many of their funerals. I often commented to people that someone needed to build a truck driver memorial to remember the drivers – they keep our county going.

I started saying that in 1980. It's not until you live in the outback, that you fully register how important trucks are to you, every day of your life. It's the same across this vast country, trucks are important to everyone.

While living in Normanton there was a short supply of people who were a Justice of the Peace. I was asked by the local police sergeant to become a Justice of the Peace, and I have been one for the last 45 years.

One day, I was asked by the police to go with them to the morgue at the Normanton hospital. They wanted me to identify a body for them. I swallowed hard and went with them. To my horror, it was a friend of ours. I'll not mention his name to protect the family.

He had an accident on the Mt Isa road and had crawled from the vehicle with a bottle of Coke in his hand, to sit against a broken tree stump in the hot sun. The temperature that day was 42 degrees; he was cooked by the sun.

His family took his body back to his hometown to be buried. I once again brought up the fact that we needed a truck driver's memorial.

Living in the outback for so long, I had no idea if a memorial for truck drivers existed. There was no internet in the town then. I wanted to build a truck drivers' memorial wall; this was now in the year 1986.

As time went on, we heard of more of our friends who had been killed in truck accidents or passed away by other means. My desire to build the memorial wall never dwindled. It was too hard to do something like that while living in the outback. Our phones only had a handle on them, and you had to wind them up to get the operator to connect you to the number you wanted. Can you imagine how frustrating this was? Every time you wanted to talk to someone, you never knew who was listening to your conversation.

We built the two shops and a house on two blocks of land side-by-side, opposite the Normanton railway. In 2024 the shops are now the Centrelink office, and the house is an office – I'm not sure what for.

In 1988 we were lucky enough to go for a holiday with the police sergeant, Gordon, and his family, around the world. My mother and father came up to look after the place for us and our staff looked after the shops. It was a wonderful break. We flew to Los Angeles then bought a station wagon and drove up to San Francisco, up to Quincy, and back to California. From there we drove across what is called Route 66, which was before a bypass was built. It was a fantastic drive. We drove to Memphis and went to Elvis Presley's mansion, onto Florida. We then flew to England

and went from one end to the other, up to Scotland and down to Lands' End, from one side to the other. It was fantastic. I had a ball.

Then we went to Singapore, India and Bahrain. Then back to reality. Would you believe while we were away the council decided to do roadworks in front of our shops and closed the road. Our sales had dropped significantly. Not good, but we survived.

One day we were home, and I was about to go to our shop. Just as I was about to go out the back door, the front doorbell rang. This pulled me up, because no one could get into our house yard except the local police sergeant. Our cattle dog, Diesel, wouldn't let anyone in, except the sergeant. I wondered why he was at the house, so early in the morning.

Garry opened the front door and Gordon (the police sergeant) asked Garry to go to Croydon with him to help bring back a truck. No one in the town was available that day other than Garry, who had a road train license.

I called out, "See you later. I'll get tea ready for Darryl tonight. I've made the bed for him if he stays the night".

Darryl Holzheimer used to bring supplies from Cairns for us – he was Garry's twin boys' uncle.

I went to the shops for the next seven hours and came home to put tea on. I ended up feeding the girls and wondered why Garry wasn't back yet; I also wondered where Darryl was. They probably got caught up along the road and are still talking, I thought; that's nothing unusual for truck drivers, I was sure they could talk underwater.

A few hours later the door opened. I said to Garry (without lifting my head), "I fed the girls; they are in bed. Did you see Darryl? I have tea for you and Darryl in the oven, I hope he likes what I cooked".

There was icy silence. I looked up at him because, I blurted this out in one breath, I now saw his face: it was as white as a ghost.

He told me Darryl was in Normanton, and with a long pause he said, "He...he… he's in the morgue".

I fell on the arm of the chair, "Darryl, not Darryl," I cried. Darryl was unloading telephone poles in outback Croydon. No one in the town had cranes, so the logs were dropped to the ground from the top of the trailer. One sprang back and crushed his head. He died instantly.

Garry had to drive the truck back to Normanton. It was such a shock for us both. Darryl was family, and it was something we'll never get over. Over the years we had a long list of friends who passed away and were taken to different locations across Australia to be buried.

The list kept adding up over time, then we got the news none of us were expecting. The grandmother of Garry's twin boys was killed at the coastal mining town of Weipa. Thora (Toots) Holzheimer was killed when one of the concrete beams being unloaded from her truck swung and crushed her against her truck. We attended her funeral in Cairns.

By now we had attended seven funerals. The rest of our friends were taken to their hometowns to be buried. After Darryl's death, Normanton never felt the same.

I so wanted to build this memorial wall now. "When I leave Normanton, I'll build that wall to remember the drivers who have lost their lives." This was my regular saying.

We left Normanton because Garry kept sneezing and had sore eyes; we thought it was the constant dust. We sold our stores, by vendor finance for $750,000. They were to pay us monthly. We received two payments and then the payments stopped. I went to the solicitor we used, and he said there was nothing he could do, because the man who bought the business took everything to his parents' shop and left our shops empty. He told us that to try to fight it would take years to get through the courts and by then the video tapes and

TVs, and video machines would be worn out and long gone. We lost the lot just like that, after years of building up the businesses. I was angry because we had paid solicitors and accountants to write contracts to sell vendor finance and we lost the lot.

We sold the house and shop to cover the loans we had but lost all our profits in the business.

We moved to a little place called, Biboohra, 13km north of Mareeba, west of Cairns.

Garry started a new job carting fuel to Bamaga, Pajinka, Weipa, Aurukun, and other places around Cape York Peninsula, Karumba, Normanton, Lawn Hills Gorge, and across the Gulf of Carpentaria, and anywhere in between. He did this job for over 10 years. We ran under our company name, subcontracted for Trinity Petroleum out of Cairns.

I went on a few trips, one was up to Aurukun, Bamaga, Seisia and Pajinka – a trip of approximately 400km from Weipa. It took four days to get in to Bamaga; we were the first truck in after the wet season and Garry had to cut trees down to get through and fill in enormous potholes, to be able to carry on. Something broke under the truck and it had to be chained up.

When we reached the Jardine River crossing, Garry had to drive the truck on the barge then drive to the front of the barge, reverse back and drive forward as fast as he could, then slam the breaks on at the front of the barge, to make it move, because the water was a bit low in some spots. Oh! My heart was in my mouth; I could see us being crocodile food. I was praying hard. That was a very interesting trip – one that could make a book on its own. I have no idea how Garry did that, year after year. I asked why the river was so low after the wet season. The only answer I got was, "The crocodiles were thirsty and drank the water". Oh boy…

Garry left the job and the man who took over his position died on his first trip. He had taken his young son in the truck to

Lawn Hills Gorge. They were both killed when they came upon a freak storm. The truck before him made it to the mine. The men at the mine were waiting for this truck that our friend and his son were in, to arrive. About one hour later they heard a mighty crash.

Our dear friend came around a corner, and there was no road, a storm had hit, and the road was washed away by the fast-flowing water, after the first truck had gone into the mine. When he came around the corner he had no way of stopping, as there was now, no road. The truck went down, the two tankers stacked on top of the prime mover.

This was one of the biggest upsets for us. Garry often said, "I should've been in that truck". I told him constantly that it was not his fault. It took quite a few years for him to come to terms with that accident. The boy was so young.

They are one of the many reasons I ended up building the memorial wall, which includes their names.

Time passed and we went to more funerals for truck drivers. I helped a few of the wives in our area to cope. I looked after their children, sorted out their insurance, etc.

Garry called me one morning and told me to go to one of our best friends' houses, as he had just seen the husband's truck go over an embankment, with no chance to survive that crash.

His wife told us she had no insurance, and didn't know how to pay for his funeral. We asked our trucking friends if they would help us pay for his funeral. Together we raised over $3,000 to have him buried. Garry and I placed a beautiful Mack sign in his coffin with him – he always loved that big chrome Mack truck sign.

It wasn't long after this that yet another icon in our lives was killed. I once again said, "You wait and see, one day I'll build this truck drivers' memorial".

I went on many trips in the truck to many parts of Australia and helped dig trucks out of bogs that were buried up to their axles. I could go on about our adventures but that could make a book on its own as well.

My eldest daughter left home in 1990, and stayed in Mareeba to pursue her career as a florist. She had a boyfriend and was happy. It was very hard to leave her while we moved to Spring Creek near Gatton in Queensland's Lockyer Valley. Garry was carting general freight from Cairns to Brisbane. Our move was a big one for us. Rather funny, we had everything we owned on a road train, and the first trailer was unpacked. Garry went to Toowoomba to get the second trailer. The items on this trailer were virtually thrown in the yard. Garry had to go and do a job, trucking.

My youngest daughter Dionne, me and a friend moved everything into the new house. I think Garry was glad a job came up – it got him out of moving furniture!

I think without realising it, every place we moved, I was looking around for areas to build a truck drivers' memorial. I looked for locations where there was hardly any graffiti and vandalism. I thought if I ever get to build this memorial, it'll have to be for the families left behind.

They needed a safe place, so mums could shed a tear and not have to watch that their kids wouldn't get hit by a truck or car on the road. It was important to think hard about many important things, if I were to build it.

On 17th December 2002, my mother passed away and was buried just before Christmas. My husband's father passed away, a few weeks later. Mum was buried at Gatton; I had shifted them down from Mareeba to a home in the Lockyer Valley. Garry's father was buried at Mareeba.

We arrived home after Garry's father's funeral, with a loaded truck. I stepped out of the truck and said, "That's it, I have made up my mind. After thinking about this for so many years, I'm going to build this truck drivers' memorial wall".

I had no idea how to do this, where to start, or who to contact. This was going to take a lot of thinking. It was difficult and I was focused on supporting my father, who didn't cope well with the passing of my mother. They were married for 65 years, and he missed her terribly.

I had asked several councils in several suburbs, about locations to build the wall. I received quite a few knockbacks. I didn't give up. I was determined by now to build a wall, somewhere.

Someone told me about a park in Gatton, with about 165 trucks leaving the town per night.

I went and had a look at the park, it was just what I visualized for the memorial wall. A beautiful park, with a lake, and a gentle sloping hill. Perfect, I thought. I found the location.

I paid a visit to the council and asked to see the mayor named Jim, who told me I had to write a letter to the council. This excited me, as I didn't get knocked back.

I was finding this project extremely hard and wasn't sure if I could go through with it. I didn't do very well in school, leaving school at a young age, and my spelling and pronunciation were terrible.

I laugh a little to myself now, as I wrote some letters with dreadful grammar, but I wasn't going to let that beat me. I was determined to get this wall built, even with my bad spelling and writing.

I will add here, sadly only a few months ago, in September 2024, I found out a woman had been imitating me and writing letters to many businesses and councils telling them things like, "I should be made a patron of the wall", and "I should be recognised more for what I did for the museum and the town of Gatton, and bringing people to the town of Gatton, to help it through the drought". She also wrote one letter pretending to be a solicitor and an accountant. And she also wrote to truck companies – using my name! I was horrified to find this out. I assure you, I have never written a letter to anyone about myself and Lights On The Hill.

I approached the mayor, Jim, with my wall building proposal.

The Gatton Shire Council (now known as the Lockyer Valley Regional Council) had its meeting, and I was told I could go ahead with the wall, with some conditions.

The first condition was that one of the councillors was to work with me to help me with the council side of things. A councillor named Kevin became the council's working partner. Kevin helped me with the council side of things for a while, and he also helped look after the takings of the first few convoys that happened later on, while he was on council.

The other condition was that the funds raised were to be controlled by the council; I loved that condition because it meant I didn't have to worry about the money.

By now, I was so excited – I had the approval to build the wall. At first I argued with the council over the location. Someone would proffer it to be built at the overpass/roundabout on the Warrego Highway. I pointed out that would be a disaster, as people going around the roundabout would be looking at the wall, not the road, and where could we hold events? Not in the middle of an overpass/roundabout. That didn't take long to sort out.

Then reality hit me. What the heck do I do now? I thought.

Nearly every day, I brought my father home from his aged care facility. I had to work from home and raise awareness. How was I going to do this? I was thinking.

I had to come up with a name to register the charity. This took a few weeks to work out because it had to be a special name.

After drawing many designs for the wall, I finally settled on a design. It was supposed to look like a truck, but it didn't look anything like one. I didn't know at this stage what the wall was going to be built out of.

I wanted the main feature to be lights shining on the wall at night.

One morning, I went to attempt drawing the wall design again. When an idea popped into my head. Why not call it, Lights on the Hill?

Garry came home that night after I had taken my father home. After an operation on his ear, Dad had a stroke and was left half-blind in both eyes; his right eye was blind on the right side, and his left eye was blind on the left side. It was difficult for him; he wasn't coping with the loss of Mum and his blindness.

Garry laughed at the mess over the dining room table. Drawings were scattered everywhere over the table. I told Garry my preferred name for the memorial. He told me it was one of Slim Dusty's songs for truck drivers. I thought, darn, now I couldn't use that name. However, me, being me, I was determined to investigate this further. I set out to find my husband's copy of this song, looking amongst the CDs in our cupboards, while Garry went to the truck to look and found it in the truck for me. Now I had the information I needed. Slim Dusty's wife, Joy McKean, had written the song.

I wrote to Joy and Slim to ask if I could use the name of the song, Lights on the Hill, for the memorial wall. They gave their approval, which meant I officially had permission in writing to use the name Lights on the Hill *(Fig. 1)*.

I kept Joy posted on the growth of the wall. Sadly, Slim passed away before the wall was completed.

I designed an etching to say thank you to Joy and Slim for allowing me to use the name of their song for the wall *(Fig. 2)*.

I placed the etching at the right-hand side of the pathway going into the wall, to look like Slim was watching over the wall that he was a patron of (*this has been moved since I left, sadly.*)

SLIM DUSTY ENTERPRISES Pty. Limited

A.C.N. 001 129 826

24th March 2003

Ms K. White

Dear Kathy

I have received your letter and faxed copy regarding the proposed Truck Drivers' Memorial at Gatton. It is very exciting to think that the Gatton Council has been so co-operative and generous with their donated area for the Memorial. It will be an added attraction for visitors to the town.

I have spoken with Slim Dusty and we both would be honoured to accept the position of Patrons of the Truck Drivers' Memorial. Also, I am quite happy for you to call it 'The Lights on the Hill' etc. etc.

Thank you for the invitation to become Patrons of the Memorial, and I would be glad if you would keep us posted regarding progress on the project.

Yours sincerely

Joy McKean OAM

Slim Dusty AO MBE

P.O. Box 115, St. Ives, N.S.W. 2075, Australia • Tel/Fax: (612) 9988 3989
Fan Club Tel/Fax: (612) 9427 7779   Email: sdekirk@ozemail.com.au
optusnet.

Fig. 1: Copy of letter from Joy and Slim to Kathy, 2003.

Fig. 2: Etching to acknowledge Joy and Slim.

I asked to use that name out of courtesy. The name Lights on the Hill Queensland Truck/Coach Drivers Memorial was never named after the song. It was named from the fact that the wall was built on the side of a hill and had lights shining on it at night.

Fig. 3: Photo of the Lights on the Hill memorial.

I had the name, so now the charity could be officially registered with the Office of Fair Trading.

Coming from the outback, I didn't know anyone down in this area. A neighbour Robert, Kevin from the council and myself comprised the committee, until I could find other people.

On the 15th December, 2003, the official paperwork arrived for the charity, called Lights on the Hill Queensland Truck/Coach Drivers Memorial.

When the paperwork arrived from the Office of Fair Trading, I purchased a large map of Queensland, photocopy paper, envelopes, and some stamps.

I had only used my computer to do my family history. I needed a flyer to tell the public about the wall. I played with the computer and became very frustrated on many occasions. When I pressed a key, my work would disappear, and I had to start again.

Eventually, I had what I wanted – it wasn't that glossy flyer that I would have preferred but it was all I had, so I went with that.

I would pick my father up in the mornings and bring him home. He would sit in a comfortable chair, or he would sit outside and listen to the birds or sit with me, as long as he was comfortable.

Once he was settled, usually with his dog or cat seated on his lap (Dad's pets stayed at my place), I would work on the project. I had the map of Queensland open on the dining room table, using a black felt pen to mark the map. On the computer was a phone book on a disc – it wasn't on the internet then. Well, if it was, I had no idea.

I looked up a town on the map, then went into the phone book to see if there was anyone living in that town. I'd send a flyer to someone, either a private person or a shop, service station, or anyone who might have an association with trucks. If they didn't, they still received a flyer. One flyer went to people in nearly every town in Queensland, telling them about this amazing new truck drivers' memorial wall that was about to be built. This took three months and a lot of our money for paper, envelopes, and postage, as there weren't any sponsors then.

I received some stamps from a few ladies who had heard about what was being built. It was unbelievable how many families wanted a drivers' memorial in Queensland at the time. I used those stamps to return a thank you letter to them. They were so sweet to offer help with some stamps; it brought tears to my eyes and flooded my heart with love, knowing they had no money, but wanted to contribute to the wall because they lost a husband or a son. One lady had lost a husband and two sons.

I soon learned in the early stages to appreciate what I had in my life, and that these families meant the world to me, as do the truck drivers across Australia.

I received quite a lot of backlash, with regards to the way I was building a memorial wall in Queensland. This was quite strange as there were three built in New South Wales, so why couldn't one be built in Queensland? I was confused about that for quite some time.

Over the years, I was told many times that I had made Lights on the Hill too commercial. It was not too commercial; everything was planned to spread the word about the wall to give everyone a chance to put their loved one's name on the wall.

The job of sending out mail took months; I did most of the mailouts myself and a friend visited many trucking companies and truck-related businesses. I think they thought, 'What does this stupid woman want to do?', as I used to get some of the funniest looks.

The hardest part was no one wanted to donate to a wall that remembered deceased truck drivers, I believe because they didn't want to look like they had anything to do with drivers' deaths.

I went from one trucking company to the next to tell them about the project. By now, my fuel costs were killing me and Garry, because we were paying for the postage and the fuel.

There was the small problem of where these trucking companies were located. I was terrified of going out on my own and coming from the outback and Mareeba, and I didn't know the Brisbane area.

Solving that problem, in the years of building and running LOTH, I didn't go anywhere without someone with me. I was determined to get this wall built, no matter what obstacle was put in front of me.

At the very early stage, the only funds raised were the postage stamps, and I was starting to think I would never raise funds.

After a while, families started to contact me and offered to donate. These donations were directed to the council to deposit in the bank, and this gave me a boost to keep going. I went back to sending out flyers after six boxes of photocopy paper, heaps of computer ink, and heaven only knows how many mailouts were posted in the first three months; it left our bank account noticeably short on several occasions.

My problem was, I was so determined to get the memorial wall built, I paid for nearly everything out of Garry's wages; as I said, it nearly sent us broke.

And then news came that none of my family ever wanted to hear: my young nephew was dying of cancer.

This was heartbreaking. He passed away three weeks after Dionne and I went to see him.

I arrived back from his funeral in Cairns, and by now I wasn't sure whether to keep going. It was such a hard slog to try to get funds. My mother had passed away only six months earlier; I missed her terribly. Dad was more heartbroken very day, and now losing my nephew, my world felt like it had fallen apart.

Trying to find the strength to keep going now was ridiculously hard. I was starting to feel like a fool with some of the comments coming back to me. I had LOTH magnets on the doors of my car and often received very nasty comments from LOTH critics. I was usually able to ignore these comments, however when you are feeling down like I was, after losing special family members, to be quite honest I wanted to give up completely.

By this point, in 2003, I packed everything in a cupboard and sat on my lounge, staring into space. The strangest thing happened. My gentle, little – and I mean little – Chihuahua dog called Bam-Bam, who had pure white long fur and big brown eyes, walked past me, put his head on my toes, looked up at me, then rolled on his side. For some reason, I felt a warmth come over me, I went and pulled everything out of the cupboard and felt like I could go on.

This was for the trucking industry, and I wanted to help drivers and families of deceased drivers. I patted Bam-Bam and said, "Thank you little fella" and proceeded to carry on.

Six months after my nephew passed away, the worst thing that I could think of, happened. It was December, and my father was missing Mum. I received a phone call from the aged care home telling me my father had been taken to the Toowoomba hospital. He had a fall and hit his head. This was his second fall in the aged care home. I called my brother in Sydney and sister in Cairns, who travelled to his bedside. My brother had to go back to Sydney, so I sat with my sister Lynette, and my daughter Dionne, next to Dad. At 9.30 am on the 25th of December 2003, Christmas morning, he passed away. I have sadly battled with Christmas ever since.

It was very hard for me, as I didn't have time to grieve, with phone calls from family members who lost someone on the roads calling me each day, while I had a tragedy in my own life. I listened to them, as they were upset; they never knew I had just lost my nephew or my father.

A lady who worked at the Lockyer Valley council told me I would need patrons for the wall. *More things to worry about*, I thought. Now who would I ask? I couldn't ask truck drivers; it would upset other truck drivers who would want to know why they weren't asked. It was the same with truck companies. Questions would be asked about how and why certain patrons were asked above others.

I thought long and hard about this and decided the only ones to ask were people who helped keep truck drivers alive, by way of songs or entertainment. But it had to be songs, or poetry about trucks. After quite a few weeks, I made the choices.

• David (Slim Dusty) Gordon Kirkpatrick AO MBE, who

wrote and sang truck songs.
- Joy McKean OAM, who wrote and sang truck songs.
- John Moran, who wrote truck poems.
- Travis Sinclair, who wrote and sang truck songs.
- Anne Kirkpatrick, a singer.

Fig. 4: Patron plaque.

Chapter Four

Many months were spent researching the best product to use for this sort of wall. I found out about stone masons J.H. Wagner and Sons in Toowoomba. I wanted to build this wall out of sandstone.

I had been told about the Australian Truck Drivers Memorial Wall in Tarcutta in NSW; I was sent pictures via an email. I never opened that email because I wanted to make sure I didn't subconsciously copy anything they did.

I took my drawing to the Toowoomba stone mason, Martin, who was so polite; he must have chuckled when he saw what I drew. I told him I wanted it to look like a truck driving towards you. We talked about a fountain at the front of the wall. Martin soon pointed out the pitfalls of fountains. He told me that the pumps could break down or spouts block with dirt, and the sandstone could become green will slimy mould. I didn't need to hear any more pitfalls, after hearing that. The idea was squashed straight away.

Martin suggested selling sections on the wall to help raise the funds. *Why didn't I think of that?* I thought. Martin was so helpful. I will always be indebted to him and his team at Wagner's.

I left my drawings and ideas with Martin *(Fig. 5)*.

A short time later, Martin called me and asked me to visit to look at what they had come up with. He told me they simply pulled my design together. I was blown away by what they presented me with. Martin went through the etchings, and plaques had to be made for the foundations and the brickworks. You name it, they

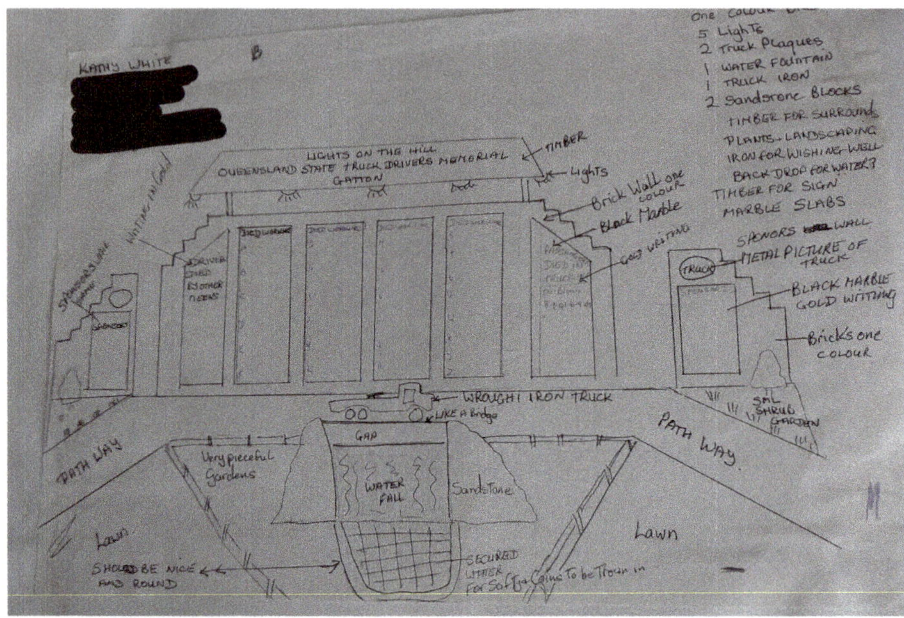

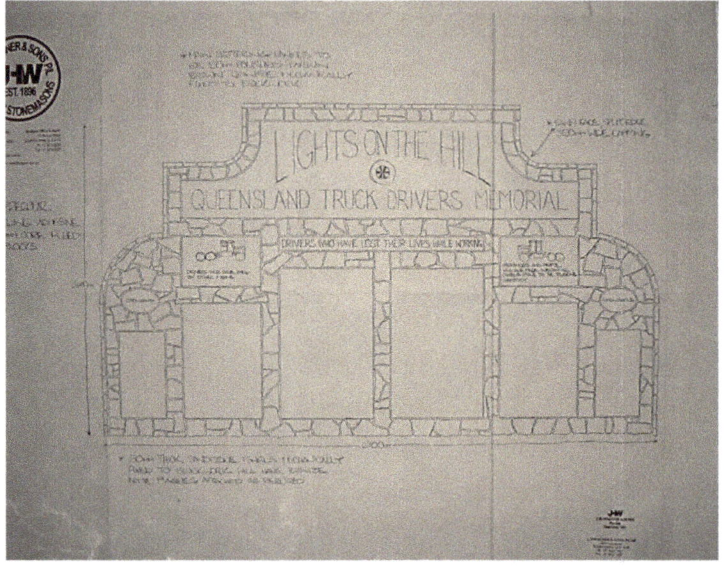

Fig. 5: Samples of Kathy's drawings for the memorial.

talked about it. I had to throw in one item which wasn't easy, the flooring. I wanted a grey, non-slip tile with a white tile for the white lines on the roads.

Trying to find a nonslip surface tile in grey was a nightmare. Once again, Martin came to the rescue. He found something, but it had to come from Italy. It wasn't cheap.

I said I would work until I dropped to get this together, and if it must come from Italy, then that's what we would use.

Now I had to take the plans home and work out the costings, to price the plaques to sell, to generate donations to build the wall. Big donations were needed to build this wall. It still wasn't easy getting support from trucking businesses.

Martin gave me a letter explaining why they came up with the products for the wall; it was beautiful.

Here are the explanations from Martin and his team.

The simplistic shape represents the front view of a truck seen from a distance ~ grille, rounded guards, lights and cabin. The choice of materials are:

Helidon sandstone

As a local material the sandstone represents the fact that many of the people in the trucking community will be the people next door, relatives, and friends. The irregular shapes demonstrate that no two are identical. Yet together they all work to get the job done.

Darwin brown granite

While this material is quarried outside Queensland. It represents the distance that many drivers travel and in doing so they bring people together. The colour of the Darwin brown granite is also a symbol of the character that is unique within the trucking community.

Bronze

The use of bronze plaques for the individual names on the memorial demonstrates the strengths and mateship relied upon during times of adversity and hardship.

I went to newspapers to start advertising and promoting the wall. This would help to find the families of deceased drivers to help them have their loved one's name placed on the wall.

I did radio interviews across Australia, placed media releases in newspapers, posted flyers to as many areas as possible. Places I couldn't reach by car, I asked truck drivers to place them at truck stops – on their workroom notice boards, anywhere they could. I worked so hard.

There was a lot of work to do now. The *Gatton Star* and *Big Rigs* newspapers were contacted about the location of the wall. A TV program called *Extra* came out to Lake Apex Park in Gatton. I had sent an email telling them about what I was going to build and they asked if they could interview me. I explained that there wasn't anything to show at the moment but they still wanted to interview me.

There used to be a little café at the side of the park, but it was pulled down when the transport museum was built. The TV show interviewed me, and I showed them the plans for the wall and the location. I was grateful for the interview that went on TV as it started to open doors to help with fundraising.

This is interesting about me. As a child I was forbidden by my parents from asking people for money, as in selling raffle tickets etc. For me to ask for money was like a huge mountain to try to get over. I found this part hard; believing people worked hard for their money, and it wasn't my place to ask for any of it, but I had to go on, so I did.

It was time for me to take the plans to trucking companies to ask for donations. Martin had given me quotes on sections of the wall that could be used to help raise funds. I worked out how much to add to them to help with donations.

I went out almost every day to ask for donations but it was like hitting a brick wall for a long time. I sold sections of the wall to trucking companies. I held the first convoy to help raise the $25,000 needed to buy the roadway tiles around the wall so we could start the building of the wall. After the first convoy's success, companies and people realised that what I had started was working. A lot of material items, such as caps, stubbie holders, bags, shirts and items sporting company logos helped at convoy auctions to raise funds.

My fuel bill, and phone bills, had gone through the roof. I was taking the funds out of Garry's wages to cover this. I didn't want to use the funds being raised because the donations were quite small, and they were starting to build up by being left in the bank. I felt worried about taking any money out for the fuel and phone bills from donation money.

After the first convoy, families and friends of truck drivers started to donate a little more, and so did companies that had lost drivers.

It was time now to try to sell the etchings on the wall. I was excited about approaching some companies with the plans for the wall. I showed them how they could donate by way of purchasing a beautiful granite etching.

I approached Mack Trucks, Brown and Hurley, Nolan's Interstate Transport, (Darren from Nolan's asked Lindsay Transport to donate for me.) Janke Australia, Gearbox Services and Volvo Trucks, to ask for donations. These companies donated towards the etchings on the wall and the roadway and flagpoles to be erected.

I went to many companies asking if they would like to donate anything to the wall. Sadly, many turned me down. After a few months of visiting companies, I was getting weary, as I felt my life was now being run by LOTH. I started to get sick and was told by my doctor I needed to slow down.

It took a few months for me to start to feel better. I knew I still had to keep going as it was important to keep those funds coming in. Donations were sent directly to the council to be banked; I went to the council every time I received a cash donation (that was quite rare but it did happen). When money tins had been placed at service stations or roadhouses, the tins were returned to the office. I made sure someone was with me when it was opened, then counted and banked. I was uncomfortable handling donations, having grown up not wanting to ask people for money. It was not a good place for me; it was unfamiliar territory and it made me be extra cautious as I felt I was under scrutiny because there had been critics upsetting me when I started .

It was amazing how many donation tins were stolen from service stations. No one could believe people would steal from charities, but they did. I stopped this practice and asked everyone to bring their tins into the office. It was wrong that people were donating to the truck drivers cause from the goodness of their hearts and some horrid people were stealing that money. It also upset the wonderful people who had placed the tins in locations for LOTH.

A songwriter named Kelly Dixon came to find me. He used to drive trucks and was now a farmer writing songs and bush ballads. One of the famous songs he wrote is Slim Dusty's song called, *Leave Him in the Long Yard*. A beautiful song.

Kelly offered to help me raise funds with a concert at the back of the Commercial Hotel in Gatton by organising the artists. It was a small area, so it wasn't advertised very much. There wasn't much room to put too many people in the area.

The artists who donated their time to hold this concert were:

- Kathy Sunners
- Lance Ellis
- Johnny Kaye
- Kelly Dixon
- Mike Hearn

- Dean Perrett
- Craig Keating
- The Kowaltzke Family
- John and Judy Stephenson

I met a man named Ian that night. He became one of LOTH's best supporters and an Honorary Life Member. After the wall was built, Ian was at every event with me and my family. He found items to auction and asked trucking companies for the use of their mobile BBQs and marquees etc. He passed away in 2016 and is still sadly missed by our family. We had Christmas with him for many years.

The concert went very well, and everyone had a good time; this was the start of the fundraising ventures.

Three CDs were donated to LOTH. Sadly, one couldn't be used due to legal problems.

I met a family named Williamson. The wonderful Mrs Williamson was kind enough to lend me a large amount of money to buy merchandise to sell to help raise funds.

A few people said merchandise use would make the venture too commercial.

But everywhere I went, people asked if they could buy hats, shirts, or merchandise – they wanted to donate but also wanted something for their donation, hence the merchandise.

I went down that path and it was a huge success.

The logo had to be designed for this project. This would be interesting, I thought.

Back to the drawing board I went and finally picked the first logo. I asked Darren Nolan, one of Terry and Daphne Nolan's sons from Nolan's Transport, what he thought of my design, and he liked it, so I went with this one *(Fig. 6)*.

The logo was on the first LOTH shirts, hats, key rings and stubbie holders.

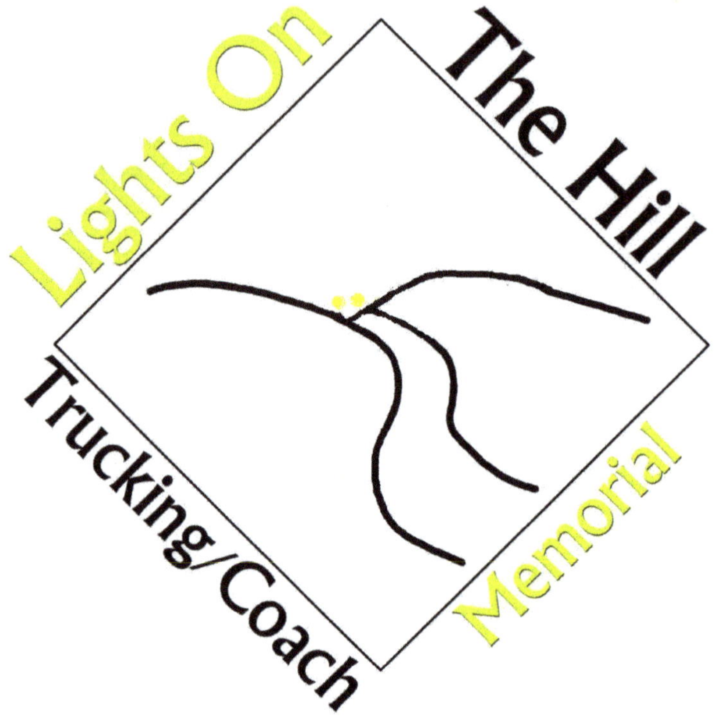

Fig. 6: Lights on the Hill logo

I raised the funds to repay Mrs Williamson and then asked if her granddaughter Taylor would open the wall. She lost her father Scott in a truck accident.

I was the happiest person in the world in 2004, *I think*, the day the council told me I had enough funds to pay back Mrs Williamson. I now had every cent of her money plus the funds to build the wall. This was the biggest relief ever.

I had worked hard to raise this money. As you can guess, I was proud that I had made it this far. The only missing items were the tiles for the road, $25,000 short.

Chapter Five

The year 2003 came to an end and I was tired. I was missing my parents and nephew. Stressed about how much it was taking out of our wages to buy the fuel etc, there was still $25,000 to raise for the floor.

I was wondering if I was doing the right thing.

A lot of our weekly wage was going into fuel. I wondered if I could carry on with the project. People were now starting to want to know why there was no wall when I was raising money. *Heck, what was I supposed to do?* These thoughts would go through my head. I was the only person doing this and I thought maybe it was time to cancel everything and return people's money; it was sitting in the bank. Fatigue had set in, Garry was away a lot, and I just kept working and didn't take time to eat, half the time. When I did eat it was usually a piece of toast with Vegemite. I was getting very run down and felt like I couldn't keep going.

But I always found the strength to keep going after a few good nights of sleep.

Gear Box Services had donated $3,500 towards the flooring.

I had exhausted where to go to get large donations, as many trucking companies still didn't want to be a part of a thing that represented death. Remember I was from the north and didn't know the names or where to go to find a lot of the trucking industries. No internet for me then.

The general public and some trucking companies were slowly

donating to the cause. Funds were being deposited into the council's LOTH account. The last amount had to be raised before I could say, "Let's build this wall".

I sat down for a few days trying to work out how to raise these funds. It had taken a lot of advertising about the wall – free advertising, thank goodness. I was talking to Ian about holding a convoy. He told me he'd heard the Convoy for Kids had been stopped years ago by authorities in Queensland and he didn't think I would be able to hold one.

Not good words to say to me. Ian put me onto a man named John, who also told me that the Convoy for Kids in Queensland had been stopped by authorities. Apparently children tried to hang out the windows of the trucks and it was tricky getting them to put their seat belts on. This wasn't going to deter me, I can tell you!

I wrote letters to the Premier, the Police Commissioner, and local police. I received so much support from them, it was astounding.

Gosh! Panic set in, *how the heck do I do this?* I thought. I was sure I was going to do this convoy because it was to raise the much needed, remaining $25,000 in funds. I called Nolan's Transport and a few other trucking companies throughout Queensland to determine the best time of the year to hold a truck event. It was decided February was the quietest.

My thoughts were to hold a convoy at the beginning of the year, once I was told February was a good time. This would be a wonderful day for the drivers and families to get together to just enjoy the day and catch up with each other, free from talk of deaths. *Let them just enjoy themselves*, was my plan.

I decided to hold a memorial in October when it seemed other truck memorial organisers held theirs in October as well. I spoke to one person who was running one of the NSW memorials and he told me that we would make October a National Truck Drivers'

Memorial month.

I felt that this was a time to remember the drivers no longer with us. I was happy to have two events separated, after asking many questions of drivers and family members to see what their thought were.

The date was set for a convoy to raise those last funds. Next was the event plan for submission to the police event team. I had to find an insurance company to insure the event – and what a job that was – and I was relieved when that was sorted out.

As this convoy was the first time I have ever had to organise an event this big, my only thoughts at the time were centred on raising the full amount needed to buy the tiles for the flooring so the wall could be finished. My mind was in a whirl, to sort out how to start a convoy event. Boy was I nervous and extremely tired.

Every third day I was driving the length and breadth of South East Queensland to top up flyers; night and day I spent working on the convoy.

John advised me to only let trucks leave Brisbane, and I replied that the convoy was for people to attend from two directions. I didn't want truck drivers having to drive to Brisbane from Toowoomba or further afield. I planned to have the convoy departing two directions.

I came up with the idea of placing a banner on the front of the truck for a deceased truck driver. This was the first time this had been done anywhere, I believe. I thought it was a great way to remember a mate or family member in a memorial convoy. I called a few trucking friends and asked them if it was possible to drive a truck with a banner attached over the front of the truck. They jumped at the idea and the banners were born (in Queensland, anyway – I have no idea about other states). I got the idea from one of my drawings. I had drawn a Mack truck and drew a banner of a child across the bull bar. I thought, *what a lovely way to remember deceased drivers*.

I organised entertainers with the help of artists Kathy Sunners and Kelly Dixon.

Then I made flyers on my computer, and with a friend, drove from Gatton to Sunshine Coast, Gold Coast, Crow's Nest, Toowoomba, Coominya, Warwick, Yamanto, Ipswich, and any place in between. Leaving flyers in service stations, even in caravan parks, and anywhere else I could find to post them.

This took weeks. I paid for the fuel for these trips. Some truck drivers distributed flyers further afield. This helped. These flyers went to places I couldn't get to.

I stayed up night after night, sorting things out. I had a list of things that had to be done. The venue was sorted – it was to be at the base of Lake Apex Park in Gatton.

The day before the convoy, Garry took the day off work to help me pick up marquees, etc. Ian picked up BBQ trailers from Brown & Hurley and Mack Trucks to use. John O'Brien Toyota at Gatton was terrific – for years they lent their large red marquee and supplied me with a car whenever I wanted one. Nolan's helped with the stage (flat-top trailer). The food side was organised with local charities, which was done by the Endeavour Foundation and the wonderful Kylah family from Gatton. The Lions would operate the bar. Artists donated their time to help.

My focus was on only one thing – to make this convoy a wonderful event for the truck drivers and families. I would spend hours thinking this event was for the truck drivers and families; it must be relaxing and fun not a huge money maker. I just wanted drivers to come together in a totally relaxing environment.

This was nerve-racking when you have never organised anything like this. You can panic if you aren't careful. Luckily, I didn't panic, but I was very nervous.

Ian had been asking companies for donations to hold an auction, and this was a great help. I had been doing a lot of radio interviews with 98.9 FM and met Dusty Fraser, who became a great friend and also an entertainer and Master of Ceremonies (MC) at the convoys, every year I was there. Dusty did everything free for LOTH and for the truck drivers. I was grateful and proud of him; he was made an Honorary Member of Lights on the Hill.

The main event police worked out the routes for the convoys with me; they had to cater for roadworks. The Toowoomba police helped with the location for the trucks, to line up before departure through Toowoomba.

BP Archerfield was kind enough to allow me to use its service station as the starting point from Brisbane. Everything was in place. For the opening of the convoy, I organised a fireworks display of a truck. I wasn't sure how the wind would go. I went with it anyway. The wind was still, which meant that the smoke would lull across the fireworks, and you wouldn't see that it was a truck. But I gave it a go. It wasn't too bad, I thought.

The biggest worry was how many trucks would turn up. We had no idea. The police needed to know how many trucks were expected, for the event plan, but how do you know how many will come, when no one had held a convoy for years? The date for the convoy was now set for the 1st May 2004.

The morning started early with help from Garry and Ian and his vintage truck club friends who came to help. A few other people popped in to help – Allan and Rose from Mareeba, who were old friends.

The marquees were set up the day before. On the day, Endeavour and Lions' helpers came to help with their stalls, as in the food and bar area.

I had organised children's events as well. A wonderful trucking family looked after the children for us. I can't mention their name without their permission, sorry.

I also made myself a promise that I would stand at the entry and wave to every driver who came in the convoy, to say thank you for coming. I did this the first time and every year since then.

On that first day when I realised 89 trucks were coming, I was so pleased. They rolled in and were parked up, and the day started. It was fantastic. I can't tell you how excited I was that drivers had come from so far to be a part of this.

The truck that Garry drives was parked in the location where the wall was to be built, so everyone could see it.

The day seemed to have gone very well. Sadly at these events I was so busy making sure everyone was safe, and everything was going well, I hardly got to meet anyone. That was through each event over the years. I must admit here I was quite scared to be around so many people – sometimes I would spot someone who looked a little like my ex-husband and my insides would panic.

It was now 1.30am and most of the trucks had left. There were still some in the park, with drivers going to sleep there. I realised I hadn't eaten or gone to the toilet from 5am on convoy day. My family went to get me something to eat. I came back from the toilet and sat down and said, "I'm glad that is over, I'm buggered".

Two men standing behind me said, "Over, over, we'll be back next year". One of these voices was Allan, who came from Mareeba to help. Other volunteers were helping as well, and I was so grateful to them.

People popped in and gave out watermelons and people I'd not met were helping wherever they could. It was wonderful. I never got to thank them personally, but I did when I was on stage, thanking everyone.

After I had one-and-a-half hours of sleep it was time to clean up. Garry, Ian, Dionne and I, plus a few other people, cleaned up. While we were there a lady approached and said, "Kathy, thank you for yesterday. My husband was killed two years ago and my children miss the trucks, and this has allowed me to bring them to see the trucks again and be a part of the family we miss".

Those words were the start of the annual Memorial Convoy.

I realised this convoy was more than a fundraiser to build the road, it was an important event for the trucking industry.

Hence the start of the annual convoy, with the banners on the front of the trucks.

I now had enough funds to finish building the wall, and the merchandise loan had been paid back in full.

After the second convoy another lady came to say thank you, telling me her husband died and she could now take her kids to this event, saying "They get so excited to be around the trucks again – we will look forward to this event every year".

My thoughts on how to do the convoy must have worked. To receive that wonderful compliment at not one but two of the convoys, I now knew for sure that I was helping families.

Kevin, the wonderful man and my council partner, told me we had the funds to build the wall. You have no idea how I felt that day. I think if I had been hit by a bus, I wouldn't have felt it. It would have missed me because I was floating, I was so thrilled all my hard work, worked.

Kevin was working on the plans with the council, which would build it.

I was asked by the artists Kathy and Lance if I would like to go to Tasmania with them to be their manager for the trip at no cost to me – they were singers and were touring Tasmania. I had so many people ask me to build a memorial in Tasmania that Kathy and Lance thought it would be a good opportunity for me to go and have a look at the place. I would be their manager, come roadie. I helped set up the stages for them, collected their money, booked the next venue etc.

I asked Kevin his thoughts on this and he told me to go and that the wall would probably be ready for the opening when I returned. Luckily I had been working on the opening for over six months, so I felt I was safe to go.

I was now planning to go to Tasmania.

Chapter Six

Meanwhile, the council arrived at the site to turn the first soil for the foundations. I was there along with one of the patrons and his wife, John and Margo Moran, and Merle, a lady who had lost her husband. They all collected some of the dirt from the very first dig in the ground and when the bricklayer started, he gave me one of the bricks. I wanted to have something to remember this wonderful day. I wasn't going to miss this event. I was asked to climb in the cab of the backhoe and the *Gatton Star* newspaper photographer took a photo to mark the event.

Kevin from the council had helped me so much; he made sure the building permits were correct and made sure the payments were made to the council for their work. The council provided the labour for the foundations and took the money for it out of the funds that were raised.

It was lucky council also had a bricklayer in their employment, who did the brickwork for the actual wall; once again, this was paid for from the funds raised.

I still have some of the first dirt that was in that bucket and the first brick and flags that were put on the flag poles. They will be donated to a museum one day. I was at the wall to see the foundations built *(Fig. 7)*.

The wires standing up in the images were the supports for the Besser bricks that were later lined with sandstone.

I went to Tasmania while the wall section was being built.

Fig. 7: Kathy with the driver as he dug the first soil to start the memorial wall build – a newspaper clipping from the Gatton Star.

Kevin was there to make sure the works were carried out *(Fig. 8)*.

By the end of the trip, I felt like I could take on a job with a big band doing that sort of work. It was fun.

I went with them to Tasmania to promote the wall down there. I had so many phone calls from Tasmania asking me to go

Fig. 8: Action shots from the start of the build.

down and build a wall in Tasmania. Kathy and Lance sang *Lights on the Hill* at every event they went to around Tasmania. I said I didn't realise just how many people dress like Slim Dusty. I had so many people come to me who just looked like Slim, telling me they loved what I was doing, and that they wanted me to build a truckies wall in Tasmania.

At one of the events that trip, 11 men dressed how Slim used to dress — same hat as Slim — and they came to me to talk. I must admit I was a little shocked at what was happening; they were so nice, every one of them.

On the way back from Tasmania, Kathy and Lance came up with the idea of a CD for LOTH, to help raise funds. There were a lot of discussions about this subject in the car from Tasmania to Gatton. Kathy and Lance knew a lot of artists who would donate a song for the CD, and I would contact artists to ask if they would help. We were in constant conversation about artist names and songs that would be appropriate for a truck CD. That year of 2004, I was invited to do radio interviews across Tasmania.

Returning from Tasmania, I discovered the wall was almost complete. Excitement set in for me to see the wall standing there. I was glad I was away during its construction, as it was such a nice surprise to see my hard work become this beautiful monument.

I thought if I saw the last part of the wall being built, it wouldn't have had that amazing impact on me when I saw it.

The stone masons from Wagner's came down from Toowoomba and placed the sandstone on the wall. The centre of the wall comprises Besser blocks. Wagner's team placed the sandstone on the front of the Besser blocks. The plaques were placed on the sandstone and then covered, which stayed on until opening day. That became the foundation part of the wall.

This is what I found on my return from Tasmania *(Fig. 9)*.

Everyone who attended the first convoy should be proud to know that their entry fee at that convoy helped to have the floor finished in time for the opening. Thank you.

The council donated the roadway around the memorial and the gardens.

Garry made the fountain and stacks for the front of the wall. The original fountain was to flow over the front of the wall where the Mack truck is situated. However, after many discussions, between Martin from J.H. Wagner's and Sons and me, this idea was squashed because of high costs and problems that can happen with water fountains. Garry scaled it down to a wheel and two stacks.

The water trickled over the wheel on memorial days *(Fig. 10 and 11)*.

Fig. 9: Images of the completed memorial wall.

Fig. 10: Images of the completed memorial wall.

Fig. 11: Images of the completed memorial wall.

I had to work out which plaques I would use for sections for the Diamond Sponsors. I decided gold and silver etchings would go under the Lindsay Transport etching.

Diamond Sponsors
    Brown & Hurley's Kenworth trucks
    Gatton Shire Council
    Gear Box Services
    J.H. Wagner & Sons
    Jerrett Transport
    J. Wright
    Lindsay Transport
    Lockyer Designs
    Mack Trucks Australia
    Nolan's Interstate Transport
    Volvo Truck and Bus

Gold Sponsors
    Rentco

Silver Sponsors
    B & L Brock
    Bridgestone Australia Pty Ltd
    Brown & Hurley Group
    CLC Produce
    D&B Cross Family
    Daimler Chrysler
    Gatton RSL Services
    NTI Pty
    PLA Enterprises
    Truck it Right

Mack Trucks

Gary from Mack Trucks worked with me. Gary was wonderful with his support for many years. He offered to provide a stainless steel truck structure for the front of the wall, plus donate for one of the etchings on the wall.

The image above shows the truck that Mack Trucks donated for the front of the wall. Originally this part of the wall was to be a fountain, but that didn't go ahead. The fountain became the wheel and stacks.

The beautiful words 'In honour of those truckies whose trips ended too soon' are carved on this truck structure.

Brown & Hurley

Brad from Brown & Hurley worked with me to organise this donation. Brad was wonderful with his support for many years. He organised the Brown & Hurley plaque with the truck etching.

Lindsay Transport

Lindsay Transport donated the plaques that identified the Diamond, Gold, and silver sponsors on the wall *(Fig. 12)*.

Nolan's Interstate Transport

Nolan's donated towards the plaque for the fathers and sons, and children killed in truck accidents, and truck drivers and their passengers killed together. These names have since been removed from the foundation plaque and have been placed somewhere else on the wall *(Fig. 13)*.

Fig. 12

NOLAN'S
INTERSTATE
TRANSPORT

DRIVERS AND PASSENGERS

Peter Justin Troy
CLIMAS
"Porky"
Rockhampton Qld
Born 11-9-1974
Passed Away 17-6-2002

Passenger
Kaitlyn Louise
CLIMAS
"Bubba"
Rockhampton Qld
Born 9-3-1996
Passed Away 17-6-2002

Evan Trent
BEHRENDORFF
Townsville Qld
Born 11-11-1965
Passed Away 9-12-1996

Passenger
Jacob Ernest
BEHRENDORFF
Cloncurry Qld
Born 1-6-1991
Passed Away 9-12-1996

Noel Frederick
ALLEN
Tinana Qld
Born 16-7-1947
Passed Away 19-9-1974

Passenger
Glen Leslie
ROUTLEDGE
Maryborough Qld
Born 20-9-1941
Passed Away 19-9-1974

Passenger
Timothy Reginald
ANDREWS
"Timmy"
Nanango Qld

Passenger
Allan George
McFETRIDGE
Logan Qld

Passenger
Tony William
TILLACK
Gatton Qld

Fig. 13

Gear Box Services

Gear Box Services donated a portion towards the roadway.

Volvo Trucks & Janke Transport

Volvo Trucks and Janke Transport donated a flagpole each.

I was thrilled with this help. The two oval granite pieces were to say thank you to two wonderful people who helped with fundraising.

This etching featuring the late truck driver Greg Wright's family was to say thank you for the hard work helping to raise money.

This plaque is placed on the wall to represent one of the truck lights.

Greg's daughter Amanda, who lived in Claremont, Queensland, called me one day and asked if she could busk in the streets to help raise funds. Amanda told me that when she was young, her father, who was a truck driver, had died.

I was only too happy for her to do that, if she was safe. Only a few weeks later, Amanda handed me $2,500.

Mrs Williamson

Mrs Williamson has her son's name on the wall, and kindly lent me many thousands of dollars to purchase the first order of merchandise to sell to help raise funds.

I did it, I raised the funds to build the Lights on the Hill Queensland Truck/Coach Drivers Memorial.

CHAPTER SEVEN

Next, I was off to Kathy and Lance's studio in Esk, to help put the first official CD together. A lot of work goes into this sort of thing.

Lights on the Hill's Official CD
WE WON'T FORGET YA, MATE - Volume 1

The first CD released was offered to the charity by Kathy Sunners and Lance Kelly on their way back from Tasmania.

I went to their studio at Esk in South East Queensland on many occasions to work on the CD, and I wrote to artists asking if they would donate songs. Amanda Wright came down from Claremont and put a few songs on the CD.

Artists who donated songs were

Lance Ellis - *Detour*

Kathy and Lance - *Lights on the Hill - He Waits For Me - We Won't Forget Ya Mate*

Kelly Dixon - *Gilligan*

John Williamson - *Truckies' wife*

Travis Sinclair - *Still riding that line*

Mike Blundell - *Down the road*

Amanda Wright - *Hear Me - Daddy's Girl*

Michael and Pat Pincott - *I'm Married to My Bulldog Mack*

Neil Duddy - *Copperhead Road*

John Moran - *The Ghost of Cunningham's Gap*

Bart Thrupp - *Mick the Cattle Buyer*

Graeme Jensen - *Lonesome Highway*

Jim and Di Ellis - *Teddy Bear*

Dean Perrett - *Back to the Bush Again*

This CD was compiled at the Reel Audio Productions 2004 Studio at Esk, Queensland by Kathy Sunners.

The Second CD
WE WON'T FORGET YA, MATE - Volume 2

Lea Enchelmaier - *Remembering our Truckies*

Travis Sinclair - *Sons of the Road*

Kathy Sunners - *Gypsy in Redwings - Turbine Truckie - On The Road Again - We Won't Forget Ya Mate*

Michael Pincott - *The Old Tin Roof*

John Moran - *The Scrub Runner*

Tate (not real name) Wagner - *Six Days on the Road*

Peter Edwards - *Boppin The Blues*

Heather Botica - *Freight Train Yodel*

Dionne White - *Ghost in this House*

Paul Costa - *I'm Bringing Home Good News*

Kelly Dixon - *The Mungindi Girl!*

Paul Denman - *Folsom Prison Blues*

Jayne Denham - *Chick Ute*

Michael Pincott - *Hen house Blues*

This CD was recorded under the name Rendition Records 2010 at Esk, Queensland by Kathy Sunners.

Sadly, Kathy Sunners passed away in 2013. She was a great friend of Lights on the Hill and a huge supporter. Kathy Sunners took all the time in the world to produce these CDs for me, to sell through LOTH to help raise funds.

I was trying to organise a thank you concert and invite the artists who donated songs and poetry for the CD but sadly I ended my LOTH association before this event could happen. I will always have Kathy Sunners in my heart, for what she did for the truck drivers and their families. I was at the studio with her for many hours and was quite surprised at how much work went into producing one of these CDs, and Kathy Sunners kindly never charged a cent for any of it.

Thank you, Kathy Sunners, may you Rest in Peace.

Chapter Eight

A few people raised funds doing their own events over the years.

On the 4th of July, 2004, Joyce Gegg from Goulburn, NSW, held a luncheon to raise money for LOTH. Joyce lost her loved one in a truck accident and wanted to help raise funds. Joyce organised and cooked for the luncheon, and she filled orders for bride's dresses and bridesmaid dresses for her business as a dressmaker. Joyce was 76 years old at the time. What an amazing woman. She also sewed beautiful pillowcases to raffle or auction at the convoys.

Marian and Kelly Dixon held a concert at the Commercial Hotel, Gatton to help raise funds.

A wonderful lady out west handed me some Coke cans full of $2 coins. People were so kind to help in many ways to raise funds.

Gary Gale was a hero, Gary rode his push bike 750 kilometres from his hometown of Inverell in northern NSW into Queensland via Moree, Goondiwindi, Moonie, Miles, Dalby, and Toowoomba and onto Gatton. He raised over $14,000. Gary rode into the convoy on February 26, 2005, on his push bike with support from his wife Debbie, and daughters Nichole and Tiffany.

The truck drivers awarded Gary the trophy for the longest travelled.

Christine Frohloff, daughter of Mr and Mrs Bell, raised $561 by holding a meat raffle to help raise funds.

Others handed in donation tins. I ended up stopping this. I was very grateful to the wonderful people who took the time to place the tins in special places. We were very upset that the tins were stolen.

Brad and Robyn, two wonderful people, received donations of bread rolls from a bread company for the convoys.

Kerri and Paula set up at the convoys to feed the volunteers. Geoff and Kathy from a company called Truck Whisperer donated regularly and volunteered.

Other companies came to the convoys and looked after children, with games and ice creams, each year.

A few other people also started to collect items for the auctions.

I was so thankful to every person who helped at the convoys and memorials.

I came up with a fundraising idea, early on. I was sitting in the lounge looking at our small collection of CDs and decided to cut up some fabric to the size of one CD. I thought people could write about their loved one, or write a poem, on them. So I did exactly that – cut the material, found a biro, wrote on it and added a drawing. I have a habit of drawing and I have them all over the place.

I put the material on the table and thought that was a good idea, but what the heck would I do with them afterwards? As I sat back down on the couch, I flicked a throw rug onto a pillow then looked at it and thought I could ask for a gold coin donation and sew every CD-shaped square, end for end, once I got enough length. It could go the length from Brisbane to say Sydney – heck, why not Melbourne? It would be a huge promotion for the distances truck drivers travel. Then I could get them cut up and made into bunk covers for the trucks and auction them off.

I was excited about this idea and started that night to cut up about 350 square pieces of material. By 2am my fingers were too painful to keep going.

After a while, other people started to give me donations of the material already cut up; this was a big help.

Some were signed by the cast of the TV show *Home and Away* plus many other entertainers and actors who signed for me – some from the United States, others from the United Kingdom –were happy to do this for LOTH.

There were beautiful personal messages on them. I gave some patches to a young girl named Alysha who lost her father at a very tender age; she wanted to help raise funds. Not long after, Alisha handed me a lot of signed patches and raised quite a lot of funds.

A wonderful couple in Gatton, Mr and Mrs Bell, also raised a lot of funds, over $300 in a few days, by door knocking around Gatton selling the squares.

Other people helped with this project. It would have been great to have been able to see it completed and the trunk bunk quilts sewn up. Sadly, that never eventuated.

When I left LOTH, some of these patches were out being sewn together, others were out still with people to raise funds. I was told that the ones left in the office when I left ended up in a skip bin. This broke my heart. It was a shame – as people paid a donation for these patches. Very sad indeed.

Chapter Nine

Official Opening of The Wall

The wall was officially opened on the 8th October, 2005. Its design was the shape of a truck – carefully placed to represent what the wall was about, to remember truck and coach drivers.

The plaques were placed on the wall to look like the grill of a truck. Two of the granite etchings – Williamson and Wright families – were placed to look like the lights of a truck. And the flag poles represented the stacks of the truck *(Fig. 14 and 15)*.

The First Service at The Wall

The first service was a hard one for me. I had spent weeks sorting out how I wanted this to go. It was about the deceased truck drivers' families and friends. I felt I had to put everything in place for them.

I was told I had to do a speech. Oh my, I didn't want to do that speech but knew I had to. I had a lady named Denise Crawford on standby in case I couldn't do it.

I convinced myself to do this.

Kevin and I were putting a cover over the opening plaque. I needed a little help and I heard a voice say, "Daddy". I looked around the wall to see a tiny little girl dressed in a blue dress with a white bow in her hair, who was pointing to a plaque saying, "Daddy" while kissing his plaque.

That was it, I got so upset I started to shake, and knew then I couldn't talk. There were a lot of truck drivers on that wall, and I

Fig. 14: The memorial.

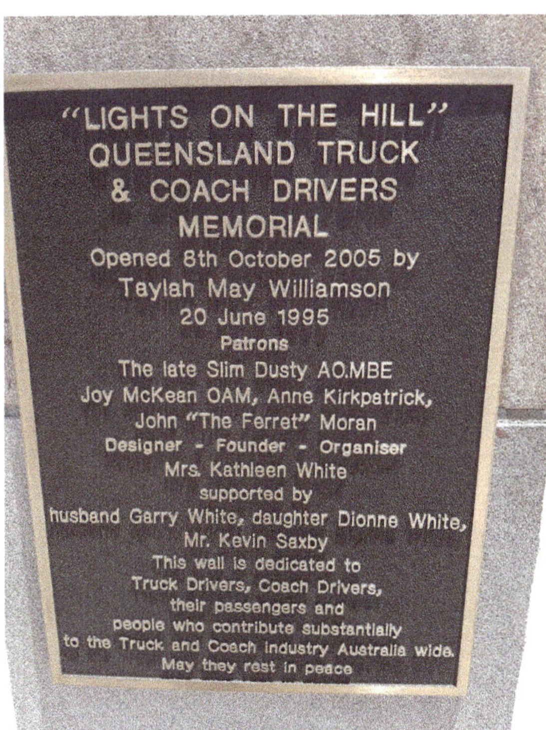

Fig. 15: An image of the memorial plaque, highlighting key contributors.

knew how most of them had died. It was heart-wrenching to come together in one day and see that beautiful little girl kiss her Daddy's plaque.

Denise read out the speech for me, and I stood beside her.

I had wanted a child to open the wall, as it was about the families – they were the important ones.

Taylah Williamson, aged 10, officially opened the wall on the 8th of October 2005. I asked that any other children who lost a loved one in a truck accident to please join Taylah as she officially opened the wall. It was so moving to see all the kids participate. After all, it was about families.

From that service, until I left, I made sure the children came up and sang the National Anthem with my daughter Dionne, when she was in the country, as she used to study horsemanship in Texas, USA. Artists Travis Sinclair and Chris Staff were there on a few occasions. I felt this was wonderful for the children, to be a part of this important event.

Fig. 16: Kathy White on left, Denise Crawford on right.

Guest speakers

Fig. 17a: L-R Denise Crawford, Ian Pearse.

Fig. 17b: L-R Kevin Saxby Neil, (Dusty) Fraser.

Fig. 17c: Nyree Feeney, Garry White.

Fig. 17d: L-R Merle Gardener, Betty Brock.

Fig. 17e: L-R Kelly Dixon, Amanda Wright.

Fig. 17f: L-R Mayor Steven Jones, Sharon Harvey.

Fig. 17g: L-R Geoff Smith, Father Louis Samyia.

Fig. 17h: L-R John Moran, Mick Bowden.

Fig. 17i: L-R MDarren Hoskins, Lea Enchelmaier.

Fig. 18: John Wirth. Lone Piper for the day, who walked past the trucks playing Amazing Grace. Each truck driver turned their lights on. As time went by there was also a piper called Joe McGhee.

Fig. 19: Dionne White (Photos from different years).

Fig. 20: Dionne sang the National Anthem with the children each year she was in the country.

Fig. 21: Opening day flowers for the Memorial Wall.

Fig. 22: Lea Enchelmaier.

Lea Enchelmaier and her husband, Ivan, came to every convoy and memorial from 2005 to 2011, the year I resigned.

Lea read out poems to entertain at events, donated artworks for the auctions, and wrote the following Truckies Prayer. This prayer was to be placed on a plaque and attached to the wall. Sadly, this wasn't done after I left.

REMEMBERING OUR TRUCKIES

As we look out and see the lights on the hill
I ask you to take a little time if you will
To remember those truckies who gave their lives
And spare a thought for their families and wives.
For our Australian trucking industries
Is surely the backbone of your great country
Hauling produce, merchandise, feed, and stock
The trucks roll on around the clock.
From Adelaide to Alice on the Darwin run
From Sydney to Perth across the Nullarbor they come
These truckies are a breed of their own
Like our Aussie swaggies they are born to roam.
The truck stop is always a very welcome sight
As they drive thought daylight well into the night
They know the roads like the back of their hand
And with pride they travel across the land.

Climbing Into the sleeper for a well-earned nap
Catching a little shut eye for a soon they must get back
Back to follow that white line down the road
Pushing on regardless to deliver their load.
But that rugged looking bloke behind that wheel
Has a heart of gold and nerves of steel
He is someone's Daddy and someone's son
Someone's partner a special one.

> So, let's build a wall no matter what the cost
> A memorial of remembrance of those we've lost
> And as we look out at those on the hill
> Please remember our fallen truckies if you will.

© Written by Lea Enchelmaier

I thought long and hard about who would help with speeches and read out their names at the wall.

Reasons for guest speakers at opening day

Denise Crawford – Denise was Ian's partner and my friend; I asked her to do my speech.

Ian Pearse – Ian had been helping me from the first fundraiser and he represented the overall truck drivers.

Kevin Saxby – Kevin was my helper with the council from the start of LOTH.

Neil (Dusty) Fraser – Dusty was a radio announcer and was our MC for the opening and for the next 10 years.

Nyree Feeney – Nyree represented Mack Trucks and the major sponsors up to the opening of the wall.

Garry White – Garry, my husband, represented the road train drivers.

Merle Gardner – Merle represented a wife who lost her husband in a truck accident.

Betty Brock – Betty also represented the women who lost a loved one in truck accidents. Betty had also given me a lot of things to auction to help raise funds.

Kelly Dixon – Kelly represented truck drivers; he also put together the first fundraiser at the Commercial Hotel Gatton for me.

Amanda Wright – Amanda represented the young ones who lost their fathers in truck accidents.

Mayor Steve Jones – Steve represented the town of Gatton where the wall is built.

Sharon Harvey – Sharon represented siblings who experienced loss from truck accidents.

Geoff Smith – Geoff represented truck businesses.

Father Louis Samyia – completed the service for the opening.

John Moran – John represented the patrons.

Mick Bowden – Mick represented the drivers from out west.

Darren Hoskins – Darren represented the drivers from up north.

Lea Enchelmaier – Lea wrote and read out the Truckies Prayer that she read for the next six years, at every memorial and convoy.

The hardest part of one of the convoys for us was that our daughter Dionne was in America. In 2004 we received a phone call telling us she had a horrific horse accident and was in hospital. Her head had been split open, and they couldn't tell us anything else. I felt sick all day, not knowing if Dionne was alright. I was surprised I made it through that convoy – the fear of not knowing if Dionne was going to make it was horrendous for us, but we didn't tell anyone; we wanted this day to be the truckies' special day.

When LOTH started to take on members, I produced a newsletter, which I called Behind The Wall, hence the name of this book. I wanted to keep people informed on happenings. This was the hardest thing I had to do, as I struggled with schoolwork. English was not a good subject. I was always on edge because I believed that what I was writing was not good, but as I used to say, "What the heck, my aim is to help families and drivers, not to look like I'm a professional".

Fig. 23: My sister, Pastor Lynette Dawson came to do the service for us on several occasions.

I used to see the trucks with advertising on the side of the trailers, and thought *I wonder if a truck company would do that for LOTH*. I approached Nolan's to ask if the company would like to put a mural on the side of one of its vans. Nolan's was only too happy to do this for LOTH. The Lockyer Valley Regional Council, Nolan's Transport and the Lions Club pitched in to pay for it.

Fig. 24: The side of the truck, featuring LOTH.

I designed it with the sign writer.

As I mentioned earlier, the TV show called *Extra* interviewed with me before the wall was built.

And a TV program at the time, which showcased community activities, called me and asked me for an interview. I suggested they attend the memorial day to see what it was about. At first, they didn't want to do this, until I described what it was about.

The show was called *Inside Queensland, Kathy White, Lights on the Hill* and broadcast what I had accomplished with the memorial. The program was great. It was a 15-minute show taped on one of the memorial days.

I was interviewed at every convoy and memorial, for TV and radio programs and news. I was happy to do this as it helped spread the word about the memorial for the families who had lost a loved one in a truck accident.

Another interview was with the ABC *Stateline* program in 2008 with Kathy McLeish, who interviewed me at my home.

CHAPTER TEN

In 2007, we sold our 40-acre property at Kruger's Rd, Spring Creek; the man behind us bought it. It was just in time – I had poured so many funds into LOTH, I almost lost our house.

Reality set in and we started to look at other houses around the area. Some of them were horrible. Garry saw an advertisement in a real estate window and said, "Look at this one". I huffed and said, "We couldn't afford that house, look at it – two-storey, huge kitchen, ultra-modern on the side of a hill at Summerholm," and I kept walking.

The next morning, we were getting desperate as time was running out to find a new home. I was on the computer looking through local real estate sites and I got up to get a cup of tea—I must have moved the mouse—and came back to that house Garry was looking at, on the screen. I laughed and went to move on from it, when I saw the price. It was much lower that what we sold our house for and better than any of the houses we had been looking at. I called Garry and the estate agent. We met, and would you believe at seven o'clock at night – that was the only time Garry could get there – we signed the contract, there and then. I was relieved because I had put so much money into LOTH, and almost losing our home gave me a scare. I had my mind set on getting this wall built, no matter what. I soon learned that I had to stop pouring money into the project; well I did, a little, but not much.

Garry looked at me one day and quietly said, "Try not to lose this house, Hon".

The sale came through just in time. I soon learned to be more careful with our money.

The charity work area was set up in the garage at our new house, and the cars were now sitting out in the weather.

One day I was talking with our new neighbour, Helen, and told her I wished I knew how to use the computer to create a new logo. I wanted to make it a bit brighter and add black and yellow to it, and she asked me why I chose those colours. I told her, black represented the bitumen that truck drivers drive on every day, and yellow represented the colour of the road signs. Helen said she could do that for me, hence the second logo. It was taken from my design, just made better, shall we say.

Fig. 25: The LOTH logo.

A few years later the name 'memorial' had to be changed to 'Incorporated' after the mayor told me I had to make LOTH an incorporated entity. Incorporated was added by the merchandise man who produced our merchandise.

Just after the wall was built, Sharon Andrews came on board to help me. Sharon had lost a dear little one in an accident, and she offered to help me in the office for an extended period; Sharon made significant contributions. She assisted with numerous tasks and consistently worked diligently behind the scenes. As secretary/

treasurer, Sharon dedicated many hours, days, weeks, months, and years working in the office alongside me at my home. She never worked at the convoys or memorial days as it was too hard for her, and I understood this. She was there to help count the takings and sort the aftermath of each event, as soon as the events finished. I will always be indebted to Sharon.

Fig. 26: Sharon Andrews.

Some of the projects we worked on together. One was this amazing book called, *We Wish They Were Here (Fig. 27).*

I was out one day taking flyers to service stations, and I ran into a lady who was quite upset over her husband dying in a truck accident a few years ago. I told her to go home and write down the way she was feeling, that it would help to make her feel better. Write the good, the bad, and the unbearable, and spill your feelings out. Then if you wish, you can burn it.

I didn't think any more of this conversation, until a few weeks later, this lovely lady phoned me and said, "Thank you, Kathy for guiding me to write down my story, it helped me so much".

Fig. 27

I looked at Sharon and said, "What do you think? How about we ask the families of deceased drivers if they would like to write a story, and we can put it in a book? Just think how many people we could help".

We both worked on this for over a year. We cried so much. Sharon re-wrote the stories to fit in the book, while I set out the book and placed the pictures where they needed to go. We cried with each story. It was so hard for us to do, but we got there, and this wonderful book was written.

We were very angry when one of the stories was missing from the book – the printer must have lost a page – and sadly we were unable to get the lot reprinted (it would have cost us far too much). I decided to include that story in a second book. I was about to start on the second book for LOTH when I left. I believe it wasn't completed.

I was talking to Sharon one day about how could we raise

money to buy some decent desks and computers to work on, without using any memorial event and convoy funds. We did a lot of research and decided we would try to apply for a grant to purchase these office supplies. LOTH had grown too big to cope with them. It took us months to apply for this government grant.

To submit our application, we had to obtain the exact costs of each office supplies item, including photos detailing the items. We found out about a lady in Gatton whose business focused on grant applications. We found her and asked her to look through the final application for us before we submitted our forms.

We needed items to set up a proper office with storage space and extra computers.

We applied for:
- Two office desks
- Two office chairs
- Metal storage cupboard
- Metal filing cabinet
- Three computers
- Three printers
- Large printer copier for our flyers
- Shredder
- Two stand-alone banners.

We received a $20,000 grant to buy the items, knowing that they would also be available for other charities to use. LOTH's door, on the Warrego Highway at Plainlands, was always open for the community and other charities to use whatever they needed. This happened a few times; if they wanted items printed, they would bring their own paper and put money towards the ink. I was glad to help them out. This happened at the Warrego Highway office quite a few times.

Shortly after we received the items, we were accused online of taking funds from the truck drivers to waste on office supplies. The accuser (who I identified) said I was channelling the money to suit myself. When challenged by people, I told them the audited books were there any time, if anyone wanted to have a look at them.

I explained that LOTH had received a grant for these items. It was malicious gossip, and untrue. It caused me a lot pain and suffering.

The National Transport Insurance company sent us a person to help with the charity and told us how to manage meetings, raise funds and lots more, at no cost to LOTH.

We set up two types of meetings. The management committee comprised four people – me as president, Sharon as secretary/treasurer, Dionne, as assistant treasurer and one other member (at one stage it was the late Ian Pearse).

And the convoy committee, which was formed years after I started Lights on the Hill. This comprised volunteers and members, none of whom worked in the office.

At one of these convoy meetings, I was trying to work out some fundraising to help with the convoy but didn't feel supported.

I suggested holding a car, bike, and truck show. They said, "Not with trucks". I replied, "LOTH can't hold events and not invite trucks – we are all about trucks". They agreed, in the end, that we could do that.

I asked who was going to look after what, for this show. No one put their hands up for anything; they ended the meeting. As they were walking out the door, two men put their hand on my shoulder as they walked past and said, "You put it together Kathy, we'll be there on the day".

This was happening at every event. I was left to organise everything. These people came on the day to help. I understood they worked, but I felt a little extra help on weekends or phone calls even, would help.

I approached an advisor I confided in – his advice was to sack the committee, as they were not pulling their weight.

I did this, and I can tell you, I wasn't popular, but I had to do something as Sharon and I weren't receiving any help.

I did resign at one meeting. I made it clear I was sick of doing exhaustive work while others implied they had put the convoy or memorial together. I was asked to stay.

I always appreciated that people worked, but it upset me that some people claimed I didn't do enough work. In reality, I worked for people and the trucking industry for no wages – from 5am to 1-2pm nearly every day. I would sometimes fall asleep over the computer.

Sharon and I received two forms each regarding a man and son, who had died, to include them the wall, with a note saying they couldn't afford to pay for the names to go on at that time. We looked at each other and decided there and then that we would pay for the plaques to go on the wall. Sharon paid for the son; I paid for the father. This was the philosophy with which I started the wall, and it was how I continued right until the end.

One day I received a phone call about some plaques found in a dump in NSW. A lady called me and told me they found some plaques at a dump, and they sent them to the LOTH office. Sharon and I set about to try to get to the bottom of this. It turned out that road workers had removed them from the side of the road and dumped them. We were grateful we managed to find the families who belonged to these plaques; they were returned to them.

It was a sad day when Sharon stopped working with me; she felt it was time to move on. We are still good friends today. I cannot thank Sharon enough for the massive amount of work she did for LOTH.

Christine Eggins helped me after Sharon left and was a great help, then for a short time Hope and Debbie worked in the office.

At one point I was offered an office/shop on the Warrego

Highway at Plainlands in Queensland's Lockyer Valley for only $100 a week until they could find a permanent tenant. I jumped at this because at my home, people were now turning up on weekends and night-time, and this was starting to scare me as Garry wasn't home much; I was on my own.

The final incident that made me take the office was when at 9.30 one night a lady called me and asked if I was home. One-and-a-half hours later I heard a car pull up outside the house — it was a lady with two men who started banging on the door. These people wanted a form to put their best mate on the wall. It was three hours before they left; they were upset and wanted me to talk to them.

By morning I hadn't gone to bed, so I went down to the person who owned the office/shop to take up their offer. I didn't have to sign contracts or pay bonds and I could leave whenever I wanted to, or if they found a perminant tenent. I set that in concrete and moved everything from my house to that location and it worked out well. Now I could go home and leave everything in the office, which made me get more rest. I was grateful to some companies who helped to pay for the rent.

The biggest concern about my LOTH work was the phone. I would give the phone bills to the council, and they would pay the bills for me. I itemised our personal phone calls. The council would work out the costs and I would put the money from our private calls into a charity tin. I asked the council and the LOTH accountant, plus the Office of Fair Trading, about the situation with the phones when I moved to the office. Each told me to keep it the same way.

In those days, the phone charges were by each call you made, and charged by the time you were on the phone — there were no phone plans like there are these days. I had to talk to a lot of people for a long time across Australia; some of the phone bills could add up to several hundred dollars on mobile phones.

At this stage, Sharon wasn't with me in the office on the Warrego Highway. Christine Eggins was helping where she could.

I decided at one of the memorials that it was time to thank the people who helped when it came to truck accidents. I had a plaque organised for the Royal Flying Doctors, CareFlight, nurses, doctors, paramedics and the police. I invited Members of Parliament Shayne Neumann and Ian Rickuss to attend.

Ian Rickuss presented me with a new Australian flag to replace the one on the flagpole for the event; both Ian and Shayne offered great support to LOTH, and I will always be grateful for that.

One of the most memorable moments I have of my LOTH years was during memorial day ceremony preparations.

While I was at the wall one day, a little girl of about four with long blonde hair and beautiful blue eyes approached me at the wall. She had a little piggy bank in her hands and said, "Kathy, put your hands together please and bend down". I looked up at her mother, and before I could say anything her mother said, "Please do this, Kathy".

This beautiful little girl emptied the contents of that piggy bank in my hands and said, "I want other kids to be able to put their daddy's name on the wall".

My gosh that will live with me forever.

Chapter Eleven

I was having a cup of tea with Ian one day and he told me I should take over the National Road Transport Museum and Hall of Fame at Alice Springs, if that position ever became available. I said to him it would be good to build a transport museum in Gatton, up on the old BMX track near the cemetery. I said, "You could build a beautiful café with an outside deck to look over the lake and the wall".

I asked Ian what he thought, and he said it was a good idea. I called a senior council representative to ask if Lights on the Hill could possibly build a transport museum. I explained where we would like to build it. There was much enthusiasm from the council representative.

Ian, myself and another gentleman held meetings at the town hall for three months; we were deciding on a name to call the museum (which I believed was separate to LOTH).

One night, working on a name for the museum, the council representative came in to tell us the council would take over the museum, which could then be run by Lights on the Hill. He indicated the council had funds to build the museum.

But the end result of that conversation was that I was never involved or included in the museum's eventual establishment, which hurt me deeply.

I went to the museum's opening and watched others be applauded for it and it hurt that I have never been recognised for my museum work.

Over the years I was presented with a number of awards. Starting from 2006 to 2011, they were:

2006 Australia Day Award - LOTH

2008 QTA Industry Recognition Award

2009 Finalist NTA Woman of the Year

2009 Australia Day Award - LOTH

2010 Finalist NTA Woman of the Year

2010 Inducted into the Transport Hall of Fame at Alice Springs

2011 Australia Day Award - LOTH

2011 Australia Day Achievement Award

2011 Order of Australia Medal.

When I built the wall, I was in discussions with the council to build stage two. This was to be two trucks made from sandstone. The first one was to look like it had parked next to the wall and the driver got out to look at the wall. I was going to have a street light placed next to this truck.

The names were to go on the trailer, and some steps were to go up one side, then a ramp along the trailer where the names were to be placed, then steps down the other side, so people could walk up there to see their loved ones' names on the wall.

Etchings from people who donated to the wall were to go across the top of the trailer. These were to be large enough that the deceased drivers' names were not too high on the trailer, so they could be easily seen. The second one was to be built years later beside the first one, to look like two trucks had stopped; it was going to be so unique.

The council gave me the go ahead for stage two *(Fig 28)*.

It turned out there were community objections to the original stage two proposal, and I put a new plan in place to build walls at the back of the existing wall and place names on that wall. This was completed by the people who took over.

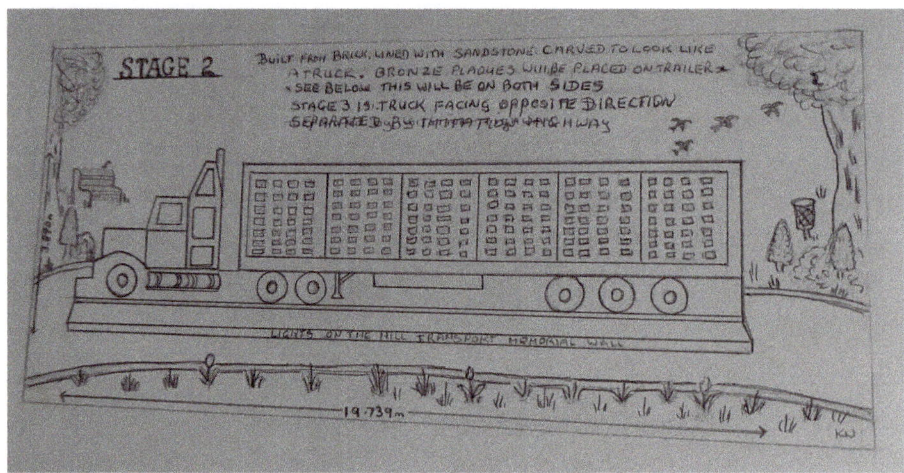

Fig. 28: My drawings of the next stages

The stumbling block for stage two arose when a lot of people became upset about potential tree removals from the lake. A new group was formed called Friends of Lake Apex. I was asked to go on the committee but I realised the odds were against anything I would try to put through, as there was opposition to anything being built in the Lake Apex park. So, I ended up resigning from that group.

I couldn't build stage two or anything in the park, and one study to council suggested the wall be moved. I was horrified and didn't hear it from anybody but read it in a report online.

At other meetings I was hearing talk of how the wall would be relocated. I was very stressed over this.

There was talk of moving the wall to a spot next to the truck stop on the Warrego Highway. LOTH members objected to this location; they thought vandals would throw bottles at the wall.

Another idea being floated was to relocate the wall to reclaimed land at Grantham, where the floods went through. I personally didn't like this location. There was enough trauma at Grantham without adding a truck drivers' memorial wall there. And there wasn't a memorial wall for the victims of the floods.

I had been made an offer for some land at the back of the Warrego Highway office, which would have been a great location. The wall could have been seen from the highway. But I couldn't raise the funds to buy that block.

The next blow came with news from the council that trucks weren't allowed at the memorial wall anymore. They had to park on the road. This made me feel very sad. To this day, I have no idea why this happened.

I heard rumours that a senior council representative wanted to get rid of me but I found this very strange. I felt as though I'd been downgraded, behind my back. When you take on a charity, you have to develop a thick skin to be able to front a lot of things that happen.

•

One day I saw a brick in my travels that had a name moulded into it. I didn't think any more of this brick, until one day, I was thinking of what I could place at the base of stage two of the wall. I thought those bricks could have names on them. My next move was to find out where to have them made. It was such a coincedence that the Slim Dusty Foundation sent me a form to ask if I wanted to put a brick at the museum they were creating for Slim Dusty at Kempsey. Wow I couldn't believe it, I now knew where to get the bricks made.

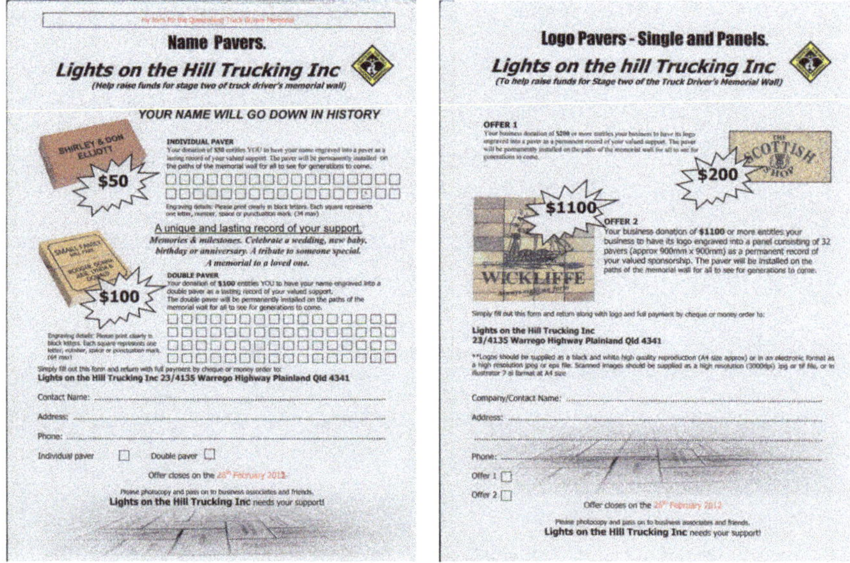

Fig. 29: Forms for the bricks.

If for some reason I wasn't going to be able to build stage two, I had plans to add the bricks beside the walls around the back and sides of the existing wall, and place these bricks around the edges of the wall.

I also purchased some cement bricks for the second stage of

the wall at a discount price with the help of Lindsay Smith, from funds I raised. There were enough bricks to build both trucks. They were to be the core of the walls and sandstone, cut to look like trucks (you will see that on the design pages for stage two). I was excited about building stage two. The bricks were delivered to the council yard for storage for LOTH, but I have no idea what happened to them.

The council yards in Gatton housed a donga that was donated to LOTH, once again with the help of Lindsay. I had helped Lindsay put his son's etching on the wall. I have no idea what happened to the donga. It was going to be fixed up as an office. It was delivered as a donation from a tilt truck company. Last I heard, it was still in the council yard with the bricks.

As the years went on, we had more trucks show up to the convoy:

2004 – 89 trucks held at Lake Apex Park

2005 – 295 trucks Gatton Show Grounds

2006 – 395 trucks Gatton Show Grounds

2007 – 450 trucks Gatton Show Grounds

2008 – 500 trucks Gatton Show Grounds

2009 – 650 trucks Gatton Show Grounds

2010 – 750 trucks Gatton Show Grounds

2011 – 812 Trucks Gatton Show Grounds.

We had some wonderful artists who played and sang at the convoys and memorials over the years, including:

- Craig Keating
- The Goodall Boys
- Dean Perrett
- Dionne White
- Dusty Fraser
- Ebony Wickham
- Jack Fraser

- Jake Sinclair
- Jayne Denham and her band
- Jeff Brown
- John and Judy Stephenson
- John Moran
- Johnny Kaye
- Kathy Sunners
- Keith Jamison
- Kelly Dixon
- Lance Ellis
- Lea Enchelmaier
- Leigh Kirley
- David Court
- Ruckus
- Mike Hern
- Neil Duddy
- Noel Williamson
- Paul Costa
- Rebecca Lee Nye and the Wild Boars
- Steve Sparrow
- Riccetz
- The Kowaltzke Family
- Travis Sinclair and his band
- The Wolverines.

And a few artists who went on stage, who I didn't know about. I was so grateful to them.

At the convoys there used to be tarp-tying competitions; Chris organised this event.

Later, Travis Sinclair and I set about to come up with a novel idea to help entertain truck drivers at the convoy. We put our heads together and came up with this event. Travis was the brains behind it, I just had to work out the finer details.

The driver had to reverse the truck using the lowest gear without stalling the truck, and when they got to the end of the line, they had to jump out of the truck, run to the front, grab an egg and spoon and hope they didn't drop it, and then run back to the truck and return to the start, without breaking the egg.

This was such a laugh, and a huge success, I set out to have this event again at the 2011 convoy, however, 800 plus trucks arrived, and the space was needed. Travis and I were going to bring this into every convoy from that year on, but sadly I left LOTH *(Fig. 30)*.

I was talking to Dusty Fraser one day and told him help was needed with the clean-up of the grounds after the convoys. I told him I had asked groups in Gatton and surrounds. A Coominya (South East Queensland) group helped one year. But no one else was interested in doing it. He mentioned his son's footy club called the Mustangs – they had used the funds they saved to give to one of the boys' family, who had lost a young son. I invited the team to help. The boys and their parents did a fantastic job. I invited them back, and they presented me with a signed photo of the team in a frame saying, thank you.

There is one lovely lady who helped, and I was greatly appreciative of her hard work. I can't mention her full name as I don't have permission to use it, but I'll name her N.S. here. Thank you.

I wanted a special flag designed just for LOTH, so I designed this flag and had it made. However, I never received them. Somehow they were delivered to a lady in Rockhampton; I had asked the company to send some to that lady and to send the remainer to the LOTH office, but all the flags went to Rockhampton. I tried many times to have them returned, without success. After I left, I believe they were on sale through LOTH *(Fig. 31)*.

I designed the LOTH flyers, convoy stickers and programs,

Fig. 30: Images of the tarp-tying competitions.

Fig. 31: A LOTH flag.

newsletters, and hand-held flags etc. At two convoys a graphic artist was used for larger flyers. My plans were to do it myself to save donated funds for the events and later for the building of stage two.

In 2005, Hawkins Transport donated LOTH a motor home to attend the Transport Hall of Fame event at Alice Springs, where Garry was inducted. I offered to promote the Hawkins' micat tours on Moreton Island, for being so kind as to donate the motor home. Roz from Hawkins Transport offered us a trip to Moreton Island, so I would be familiar with the micat tours. Garry and I were taken over to the island and spent the day there.

This was a great opportunity for us to promote LOTH and talk about the micat tours and Moreton Island, wherever we went – a promotion that worked well for us and for Hawkins Transport and micat tours.

Hawkins Transport owns the tours, with a boat that takes tourists across to Moreton Island, where they can go on guided tours around the island in 4-wheel drives.

Chapter Twelve

I received many phone calls from people in many parts of Australia, mostly from Tasmania and Western Australia, asking me how to go about building a memorial wall in their state.

This started in Tasmania. Kathy and Lance asked me to go there to help them set up for concerts around Tasmania, and in return they promoted LOTH for me. Everywhere we stopped, I was asked about building a wall in Tasmania. This was when I had only just started to build the wall in Queensland.

I eventually started the process by extending the Lights on the Hill charity to be able to raise funds outside of Queensland.

I self-funded a visit to Tasmania and went to see a lot of politicians and the road transport departments, landowners – you name it. I had to see them, and I went from one person to the other.

I can tell you Tasmania was the hardest place to obtain approval to build a wall; I understood why when I was taken around Tasmania and shown how narrow the roads were. I ended up writing letters once again to many departments, and eventually, I received approval to build a wall, subject to the location.

My next job was to find some people in Tasmania to help with this project. I had contact with a man named Marty.

I funded a trip for myself and a LOTH committee member to Tasmania, as I felt it wasn't right for wall funds to pay for two people to go to Tasmania.

I was lucky enough to contact two people in Hobart. Marty

was one of them, and he drove us around to look at some locations where the wall could be built. After leaving Marty, we continued onto the Tasmanian town of Perth, to see a man named Tristan and another named Tony. I asked them if they would come on board to help with the project.

Marty ended up leaving the project and to this day I don't know why.

After I left LOTH I worked with Tristan for a few more years with advice and letters, talking to government officials and giving my advice as to how to set up the charity.

When running LOTH, the idea was that I would help wherever I could, but they had to raise the funds to build the wall in Tasmania. The Tasmanian wall had to pay for itself. LOTH paid for the first batch of flyers for the Tasmanian wall, they were to pay LOTH back once they raised funds. I set up the charity for them to take over. I was asked how to run the events, how to go about getting the merchandise, about the logo, how to ask for funds to build the wall, how to set up plaques and many other things. I worked from my home in Queensland hard, to help get the Tasmanian memorial wall built, and invested a lot of my own time and funds into establishing it.

I had a lot of merchandise given to me to help them start fundraising, but I found out it never reached them. Apparently all were stolen from the house where they were delivered as quickly as they were put down. I was very upset over this. But there was nothing we could do about it.

I am extremely grateful to Tristan and Tony for working to raise the funds and design the wall. It was a great pleasure to help them to get to the building stage. I was pleased to learn the wall was officially opened. I wasn't able to attend the opening but I consider the Tasmanian wall a part of my legacy.

I was thrilled to be asked to build a memorial wall in Western

Australia, as I came from over there. I flew over a few times – once with my daughter to look for locations and to get approval. Of course I had to go through the same as I did with the Queensland wall and the Tasmanian wall. I went to the Northam Shire Council and they were amazing, they helped me so much.

I had found a company in WA, helping the man who had organised for everything to be donated; he had so many contacts. The wall was ready to be erected. I had been to Western Australia on two occasions – again out of my own money – to organise the project. The first batch of flyers for WA was paid for by LOTH, which was to be reimbursed from funds they raised over there.

Nothing had to be paid for in WA. I was so excited about the design. The designer did the plans as a donation, and everything else was donated – the concrete, steel, the land – so this wall was ready to be built. Unfortunately, even though this wall was ready to be built, it didn't go ahead.

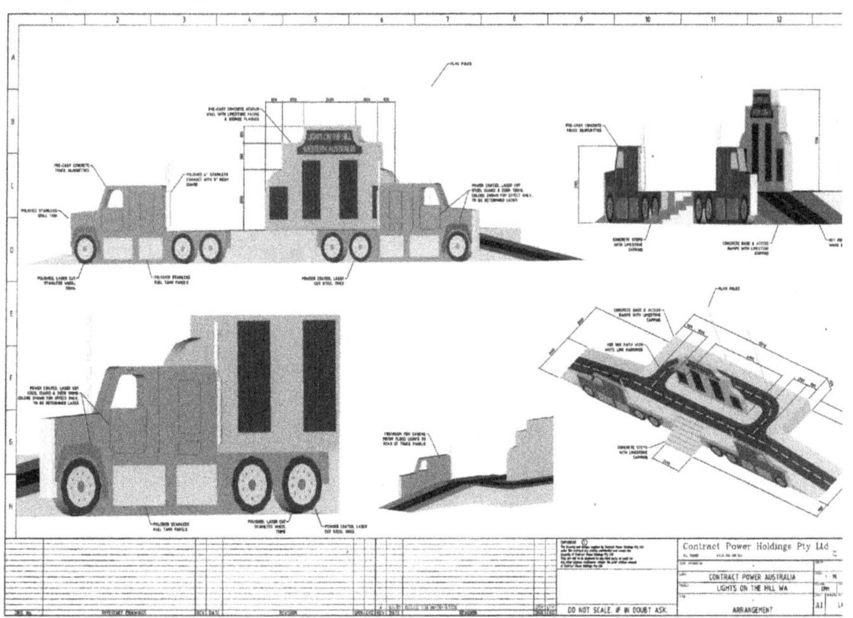

Fig. 32: Plan of the proposed WA memorial wall.

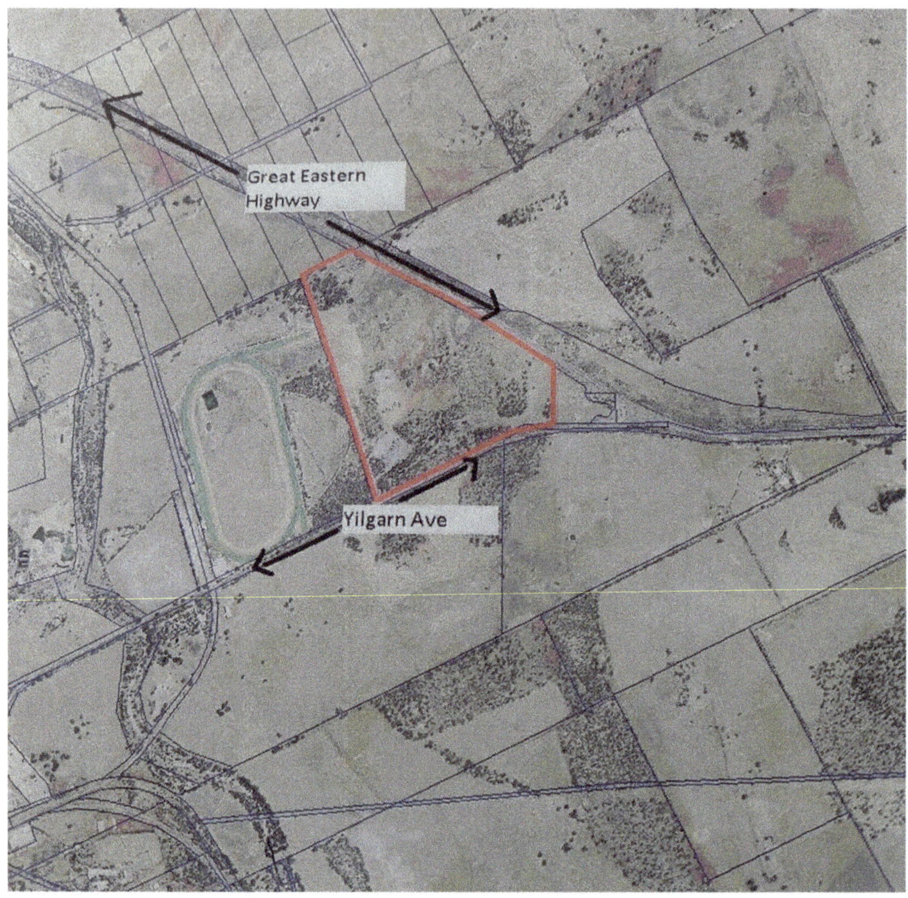

Fig. 33: Location for WA wall heading to Northam.

Eventually I left LOTH in Queensland, frustrated by the infighting. But I was still so proud of the wall, the convoys, the work over all of those years and the lifelong benefits that work gave to grieving families. Not to mention the friendships forged.

I felt memorials were important for the people – the drivers and those who lost them. Truck drivers are essential across our vast country and each state, each town, is as important as any other.

It was amazing how many phone calls I had from people around Australia, and around the world, asking me how they could go about building a truck drivers' memorial in their towns. To this day in 2024, I am still asked, and I am happy to give them advice and guidance.

I had been asked by several people in America about the wall, and how I went about getting it built. Potential organisers there asked me to go over to see a few things to do with trucks on many occasions but I felt that it was more important for me to look after LOTH in Australia.

In 2010 my daughter Dionne was going over to a world horse show in America, and I told her I would love to go with her for a break, but I was so tired. Dionne was leaving on the memorial day.

I organised the memorial day and told everyone what had to be done, and Garry was there to see it went well. I flew out the morning of the memorial.

It was rather funny, as it was my birthday the day we left, and when in the air, with the time change, it would be my birthday again. I said to Dionne, "You had better have two presents for me this year" and we laughed. But at midnight when trying to sleep on this darn plane at midnight, Dionne tapped me on the shoulder and handed me another birthday present saying "Here, Mum, this is your second birthday present, Happy Birthday, again". I laughed.

Chapter Thirteen

I had been out putting flyers around to promote the Queensland wall. I had just come back from the rural, south eastern town of Warwick – including Esk, Crows Nest, and Toowoomba, back to Yamanto and back to Gatton – a round trip, shall we say. My leg was still in a moon boot, after falling down some steps, breaking a few bones in my foot and tearing some the ligaments in my leg.

I stopped at a shopping centre car park in Yamanto, in Ipswich in the south east, to put some flyers in a store. A lady came up to me and pointed to the car saying, "What do you have to do with this?" I looked at the car to see the lady was pointing at the Lights on the Hill sign on the side of my car. I told her I built it. The lady said, "Do you remember me? I called you on the phone last year".

I didn't, as I had only spoken to her over the phone.

Would you believe the same thing happened in a café at Wacol in Brisbane the next day?

At one convoy a lady was on an overpass and she was so excited that she grabbed a man by the arm and said, "Look there, it's Travis Sinclair's truck, I can see him" as she tugged on his sleeve with excitement. Travis told me he didn't have the heart to tell her it was his shirt she was tugging on and someone else was driving his truck.

Garry and I were at a service station and a man saw the signs on the car and said, "Bloody truck drivers, only good ones are dead ones". I can't repeat what Garry replied.

A few weeks later I was at a service station putting up flyers when I came out and I was again greeted with, "Bloody truck drivers, only good ones are dead ones".

Well, I looked over at this fat-stomached man, with his shirt half open and huge red legs with bandages on them. He had a large Coke bottle under one arm and a carton of cigarettes in his other hand and a mobile phone. Out of the corner of his mouth was a cigarette that looked like it had been there for a few hours; he looked like he hadn't had a shower or wash in weeks and smelt like it. His car was filthy. I looked at him and said, in a very quiet polite voice, "If it weren't for truck drivers you wouldn't be able to buy the fuel for your car, that bottle of Coke under your arm, those cigarettes and mobile phone, your shirt and pants you have on, or even those bandages on your legs, not even your fag hanging out of your mouth. So the next time you think truck drivers are only good when they are dead, feel yourself standing in that paddock over there with nothing – no car, clothes, no cigarettes or bandages or food. Then come back to me and tell me the only good truck driver is a dead one".

I opened my car door to cheers from across the pavement, where people had stopped to hear what I had said to this horrid man.

At a shop one day in Toowoomba, a man and a woman came to me after seeing my LOTH shirt. They told me they hated trucks, that their son was killed by a truck driver. I replied, "My friend's family was killed by a car driver, and accidents happen all the time whether it's trucks or cars".

One truck driver at a service station told me I built the wall in the wrong place and that it should have been on a highway so people could see it. My reply was, "Then why didn't you build it?"

I used to receive these comments many times over the years because I was out a lot, promoting the industry. Too many of these comments to keep typing here, it would be another book.

I was at a house one day, at a small get together, when a person recognised me and started on about truck drivers. It was quite embarrassing. So, I started a fun thing with the kids, asking them what is delivered by a truck, and this went on for quite a long time; I was amazed at these kids. This rude man butted in and said, "Yar, well there is one thing truck drivers don't deliver". I said, "And what would that be?" His reply was a baby. Before I could answer, a little girl about five, I guessed, with very long blonde hair in a pony tail and wearing a green dress, white shoes and socks (she was so cute) said, in an angry voice, "Yes they do, my sister was delivered by a truck driver on the side of a highway, so there". All I could do was smile.

I had men call me for support and I was happy to do this as these men needed someone to talk to. This one evening a man called me, stressed about a fine. After calming him down and assuring him I would go with him if he wanted to go to court, he said he wished his wife was as supportive as I was. I asked him if he had talked to her. His reply was, "Hell no! She died six years ago".

One very hot day I went to a shopping centre at Plainlands, not far from the office. I was looking for a car park, and there were none under the shade.

Driving around I went to the outside area in the sun; it was one row from the shade rows. Stepping out of my car, a man parked directly in front of me under the shade yelled out, "Hey, you with the Light on the Hill shirt on, you can have my car space, I'm leaving now, I'll hold the traffic up for you". I called back, "Thank you so much, but I'll be fine". Well, this man wasn't going to have that, and he told me in a stern voice to get back in my car immediately and said he'd move his car. "Okay," I called back. He moved, I moved, and he went on his way, I went to get out of my car and a lady said to me, "That was my dad, you helped him put his brother's name on the wall, he would do anything for you, Kathy".

This made me realise just how much this wall means to people.

Another time a man called me in a very drunk state telling me he wanted to put his mates on the wall. I tried to explain that the date was closed for that year, and I would be happy to read out their name this year and place the plaques on the wall next year.

He wasn't happy with this and started to abuse me. I tried to calm him down but with no success. I eventually agreed he could place some names at the wall, but they would be taken away after the memorial because of safety.

Whenever people raise their voice at me or get abusive with me I can hear that gun go off beside my temple, that I talked about at the beginning of this book. Just like during my last meeting when I left LOTH, fear took over.

He called back the next day, telling me that I didn't care about truck drivers out west of Queensland. This I found hard to take as the truck drivers meant the world to me, no matter where they lived in Australia. Especially, considering Garry and my family spent many years living and driving trucks in the outback.

I will give him this, he did apologise, and two names were placed on horseshoes that were placed at the wall; I removed them after midnight that night for safety reasons.

I received several death threats over my time with LOTH, mainly from people facing barriers when they wanted their loved ones or mates on the wall. If the plaque-making deadline arrived, I couldn't add to it, so the name plaques wouldn't be ready in time for the memorial day.

The date was on the forms sent to people seeking recognition of the deceased drivers. I couldn't do it after that date each year and people became abusive. On several occasions, I was threatened with death for not doing it. I was told I would be run off the road. One guy was going to shoot me. Another woman was going to scratch my eyes out. Another was going to cut my throat.

Sadly, this was from people who were still grieving, so I took it in my stride and helped where I could. I lived through a few years of this, and figured some of it was only people who couldn't get things that they wanted straight away.

One death threat did scare me, from a New Zealand truck driver, who wanted his family member on the wall. I told him he missed out for that year, and I would make sure it went on the wall next year. Once again, I told this man I would make sure the name was called out at the memorial.

He abused the hell out of me. I was called a bitch, a slut, plus more names. He told me if I didn't put the name on the wall that year, he would hang me from the wall. I sort of laughed, until he said he was serious, or his next best thing was to wrap a chain around the wall and pull it down one night before the memorial service. And if I went to the police, my life wouldn't be worth living. Once he threatened to damage the wall, I got scared, I was shaking for hours after he hung up. I could hear that gun again.

The next morning, I called Wagner's and asked if they could do this one more plaque for me. I explained what had happened, and luckily, they said yes.

Would you believe, the man who threatened me never turned up for the service? He went back to New Zealand to see his mother. That was the most scared I had ever been with receiving death threats.

Another time, I had booked two people to sing at one of the convoys. One of them didn't like their allocated time and wanted it shifted. These entertainers were given this time slot to sing because the other entertainer had been donating his time singing and being the MC for the truck drivers for free for over eight years, and I wasn't going to change his time. I explained that I wouldn't change their times and I told the entertainer who wanted the time shifted that they were cancelled.

This situation landed me in court (with a dispute over airfare payments following the cancellation) and I was very disappointed that someone would take a charity to court.

Around that time a member of LOTH asked if they could organise a relay around Australia to raise funds and make people aware of the trucking industry. It would have been a logistical nightmare. It never eventuated.

This was brought up at the last meeting.

This same person who asked me about the relay wanted to start a support van – the same sort of support van that another trucking group was doing, taking truck drivers' blood pressure etc. I once again declined, saying "I wouldn't do it as I feel this is the other group's thing. We're here to help deceased truck drivers' families and maintain and extend the wall".

I told this person if they wanted to do this they would have to organise and look after this, as I was working on the memorials and convoys only.

And at my last meeting, I was accused by some people of taking LOTH in the wrong direction.

LOTH had a truck show at Gatton with the convoy, and a team of people offered to judge the truck show. They asked me many questions about how I started LOTH.

When they were asking me questions, I had no idea they intended to start another convoy. I told them that the entry forms for the truck show must come back to me straight after the show, and not to lose any. Well, they didn't come back to me and it took months to get the entry forms back. I won't say any more on this.

I was given a special award from the Queensland Trucking Association. It was the Industry Recognition Award and they asked me to give a speech. I had to decline – I wanted to, but knew I would start crying. The reason was that I had a terribly upsetting conversation with a lady who lost her son, just before I went to the awards. I used to get so emotional with anyone who called. This lovely lady told me about the heartache she was going through. I felt bad but I knew I would start to cry as my body was still crying from the details this lady had told me; it was a horrific story that would have made a grown man cry.

I was nominated for Transport Women of the Year and was a finalist. Finalists had to give a speech, and I stood up and said to the crowd, "The best thing for the industry is to have the bosses recognise the drivers, who are the ones keeping the businesses going – a nice greeting when they come in and an offer of a cuppa would be better than, 'why are you so late'".

I didn't think that went down too well with everyone. To my surprise, a lot of these business owners told me it was the best speech they had heard in a long time.

At the next awards night I told the audience about the little girl with her piggy bank (as mentioned previously). Walking back to my seat I was stopped and handed a cheque for $500 – the lovely man said he had never heard of anything so beautiful before and wanted to give me the cheque; it was the nicest donation I ever received, apart from those stamps to help get me started.

I had received several phone calls asking me to help some drivers as they had received large fines for misspelling in their log books (work diary).

I had no idea how to help these drivers who had been calling me. One day I was at my desk in the office, daydreaming at the front window. I had a large calendar under my computer for scribbling notes. I looked down at it this day and saw a message I had written from a truck driver. Underneath I had written in red biro, 'go and see the Transport Department about spelling mistakes'. I looked hard at this message. One day I must have written down how large the fines were. I thought to myself, *I will go and ask the transport department for these truck drivers.*

A week later I attended the department's offices in Brisbane to talk about the logbooks, now called work diaries. I wanted to get to the bottom of drivers getting such huge fines and for spelling mistakes.

It was rather an interesting hour. I did manage to help a few drivers with what I was told about incorrect spelling mistakes. The advice was to ask the drivers to report these incidents directly to the Transport Department. I was told that spelling mistakes can't be an offence, only if you were deliberately misspelling a place. They said the police should be able to see you have trouble spelling, by your log book. I felt that meeting was worth the effort.

Garry and I had a friend called Doc who was wheelchair-bound due to a truck accident. I won't go into detail as it is his private business. We found out his car had been stolen with his support aids in it along with the Christmas presents he had bought for his family. Garry had a ute he was trying to sell but we decided our $7,000 asking price would be much better going to help Doc. We took the ute over to his house. He was so grateful, bless him. Doc has since passed away.

CHAPTER FOURTEEN

I'm so proud of how LOTH helped people who had given so much to the trucking industry and found themselves in need. I heard about a lady who lost her house to fire, and I organised for her to receive personal items that they would need straight away. Her husband had died in a truck accident, and LOTH gave her items like shampoo, toothbrushes, toothpaste, soaps and personal items to help them get through.

A truck company lost everything in the floods that destroyed Grantham, and the owner also lost his home. His business went underwater. LOTH put $5,000 into a credit at Queensland Diesel Spares so he could go there and replace some tools to help him out.

Another truck driver, who took photos of trucks for the papers etc., had a bad leg. I found out his camera had been stolen, and LOTH sent him a replacement camera.

There are a few other things that LOTH helped with however they were asked to be kept private, so I won't mention them.

Out of my own money, I always took anyone who went with me placing flyers around or helping in some way – volunteering between convoy and memorial days – for a meal, or bought morning tea etc. to say thank you.

I paid for a casket for a little boy who died. His mother couldn't afford to pay for it.

I wasn't worried about the above, as in what I paid for; I would do it again.

What did upset me was that I heard that a man I had helped then spread rumours about me stealing from LOTH to pay for our new house – all because one day I told him that if I wasn't careful paying for everything out of our wages, we would lose our house.

I hate lies and gossip.

There were times so-called volunteers pocketed donated items for themselves – they were supposed to go to companies to pick up items donated to us, for auctions. I was disappointed to find out people were going through the boxes and taking what they wanted it was like it was their privilege.

We also had flags stolen when pulling down convoy displays at events, and photos were taken from my photo albums on display at truck shows. I am amazed at what people would take as if it was their right to take what they wanted.

I always took a wild guess at how much was missing and I would slip dollars into the merchandise banking after events to try to make up for removed donations.

Travis Sinclair built LOTH a merchandise trailer; it was used at the last convoy I held. There was still more work needed to do on it, as in shelves etc. I have no idea what happened to it after I left.

In 2011, the town of Grantham was hit by a massive flood. The floods came down from Toowoomba through to Postman's Ridge onto Grantham and wiped-out houses, and farms. The flood killed a lot of people. It was a horrific scene. We lived on the side of a hill at Summerholm and the outlook was right up to the hills of Summerset. We were now looking at a sea of water; it was devastating. As soon as the water went down far enough I went to the Gatton showgrounds to help with the cooking for the victims who had lost their homes, and for families who had lost loved ones in the floods. So many people lost their lives in that flood, it was horrendous.

The convoy was due to happen around this time, however I had to postpone it to a later date. The showgrounds were full of army vehicles, containers of clothes, food, bedding and whatever was donated for these people. We cooked for the soldiers who were out in the mud helping clean up after the water subsided; they were also recovering deceased bodies. At that time my priority was to help these people. We couldn't use the showgrounds and I sure as hell did not want to hold a convoy when so many people in the town were grieving. It wasn't like it was one or two people, it was from as far away as Toowoomba to Fernvale and beyond. I moved the convoy date.

There was one lady covered in bruises and broken bones; she was washed out of her home and hung onto a tree and was battered by fridges and couches washing past. The woman and her husband were rescued just as they couldn't hold on any longer; they were lucky.

A young girl was sitting on the end of a mattress on the floor. I asked one of the helpers if she was alright, saying she hadn't spoken a word in two days or moved from that position. I was told her entire family had died. It was a horrific time.

I was criticised for changing the convoy date that year. What was I supposed to do, tell all the soldiers and flood victims to get out of the showgrounds, that I needed it for the convoy? I don't think so.

The blessing that came out of me moving the convoy date was that not one driver complained to me. They came to me and thanked me for helping with the cooking for victims of the floods and for the soldiers helping with the clean-up; they also had the horrible task of finding deceased people. I was so proud of the truck drivers. We had a wonderful day, the day of the convoy.

I found that during the floods, so many truck drivers and trucking companies stepped in to help wherever they could. It was wonderful to see the trucking community helping people in need the same way they take hay out to drought affected areas. It makes me proud to have been a part of this great community of truck drivers and their families.

Epilogue

In June 2011, I was awarded the Order of Australia Medal for my work with Lights on the Hill.

I was proud of this achievement, not for me, but for the trucking industry. While I was at Government House that day, I was astounded by the other recipients who came to me and said they had heard about the memorial wall for truck drivers, and I should be proud of what I had achieved.

In November 2011, a person I won't name wanted to know why I was awarded the OAM, and I was told I didn't deserve it. This person told me he was going to have it removed from me.

I called a LOTH meeting that month because I knew it was needed at that time. It was an unexpected traumatic experience for me, that meeting, although I had a gut feeling the meeting wasn't going to be a good one. I won't go into the details because they sadden me but that was my last LOTH meeting.

I ended up walking away from LOTH. I felt that while I worked hard for years and achieved good for so many people, the environment wasn't good for me and it was a place I no longer belonged. Those feelings, and false accusations that were circulating about me at that time, catapulted me back to the violence from my first marriage. I had to get out of there. I could now visualise my first husband holding a knife and a handgun and I could hear that gun go off beside my head. It was scary. I literally ran out in total fear.

I had worked so hard to raise the funds, design it, and have it built. Fear can leave a person in absolute turmoil. I suffered for a long time after I left, and it took me back to the intense, constant fear that I had taken years to try to control. It was gone that day – years of hard work, gone. Journalists called me to find out the reason I left. I couldn't tell them the truth, or they would have wanted the full truth. What could I say? Nothing. And that's what I did, I said nothing. There have been a lot of false accusations said about me ever since I left, because I said nothing. I felt sorry for people believing the accusations and the people spreading them.

I built that wall for the truck drivers and their families, not for me, and I am very proud of that fact.

I had some wonderful things I still wanted to do with LOTH, and knowing they would never eventuate saddened me. I wanted to hold a large concert to thank the wonderful artists who donated songs on the CDs but now, I couldn't do this, and I found that very upsetting. I think my biggest heartache was the WA memorial being cancelled – it would have been wonderful to see that built.

My next priority was to have the prayer that Lea Enchelmaier read at every event (see Chapter Nine) put on brass and attached to the wall. To this day I am very upset that I couldn't do this, and to find out another poem was on the wall, made me even more upset. Lea had written this, especially for LOTH, and kindly drove from Yarraman twice a year to be a part of the services and entertainment and read that poem we called the truckies prayer.

These unfinished projects have left a hole in my heart. I had no idea how proud I was of this amazing project. I am very proud of what I achieved, and most of all I am proud of all the families whose loved ones are on the wall, and so very proud of the drivers' names on the wall.

I wanted so much to be at the 10th convoy to celebrate with everyone; that would have been in the year 2014. But for some reason the 10th year was officially recognised as 2012.

It was interesting to be in such close contact with people who had lost someone. I used to receive many phone calls from family members, but as time went by, I would notice the calls would get less and less. At first, I thought the people got sick of me. Then over time, I realised that they had started to move on from their loss and carried on with their life. I eventually felt good when that happened. I knew they were finding their feet again after such tragedies.

The hardest thing I found was when I could see a child suffering the loss of a parent at the wall, they would carry a little bunch of flowers and place them at the foot of the wall. It was such a tough time for me. I could never imagine losing a parent like that. I lost my parents from old age, the thought of losing a parent in a truck accident, as a child, was tear-jerking for me.

I have a wonderful photo that was given to me at one of the memorials. It's of a little boy sitting on a lady's legs, holding a little bunch of flowers. I saw this little boy when I was giving a speech at the wall one day – this photo means the world to me. He walked up to the wall, bent down and put the flowers gently down, then ran as fast as he could, to I guess it was his mother, I can't be sure. To see them just hug each other so hard, I went over and put my arms around them both and shed a lot of tears with them. I never said a word, I just held them, and when they calmed down, I squeezed them both and walked away. My heart was aching for them.

Every convoy, memorial day, and every day someone would call me about someone who had died, every one of those days was hard for me.

I had never been involved with charity work or on committees before LOTH. I had no idea about how intense and heartbreaking it would be to work in a charity.

It is very interesting over the years; I still get people asking me to go back; they tell me it has never been the same since I left.

My life has been interesting since I left. I started to volunteer at the Australian Army Air Museum at Oakey, preserving war photos. I loved working on a volunteer basis with the men who had been in the Vietnam war, volunteering with me.

The lies that circulated at LOTH followed me there, and I resigned. I decided to leave – forever – helping with anything in this format from that day on.

Garry had an operation on his foot; he stepped off the back of a fuel tanker and broke his heel. He had to have an operation to remove the chipped bone that broke off. After his operation and months of rehabilitation, he decided to retire. This changed our lives, I started to write children's truck books, and I self-published three of them. I have a pile of written books on USB sticks, and many printed in a cupboard.

I have completed a mosaic of a triple road train the size of a door, and a coffee table out of mosaic tiles, of a Mack Bi-Centennial truck on it – it's the Captain Bligh truck in my book called *The Rebuild of Captain Bligh*.

And I have completed a mosaic of a Mack truck that I framed and have on the wall in my house. I have completed many mosaics from trucks to totem poles, and mannequins. I have also won a few prizes at shows.

We moved from the Gatton area over to Russell Island for a few years and now reside in a little fishing village, with approximately 245 people living here. I am now trying to paint pictures and I am enjoying it. I find life very interesting these days.

I still miss LOTH and the families and friends of the deceased.

As much as I love the Lights on the Hill wall and all the other truck drivers' memorials, I don't want to see any more names on the walls. I want drivers to be safe and to be able to get home to their loved ones.

From us to you with much love and happiness,
stay safe out there on the roads.
Dionne White, Kathleen (Kathy) White, Garry White.

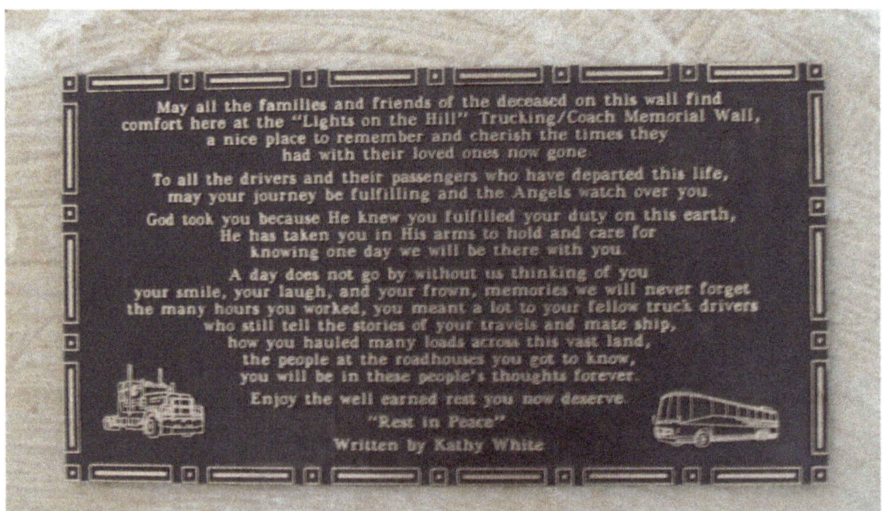

Etching situated at the Memorial Wall
This was up on the seating area above the lights, it has been
moved to a stone at the front since I left.

*Nobody trashes your
name more than someone
who's afraid you'll tell
people the truth.*

(Author unknown)